flights

of

fiction

An Anthology of Short Stories set in Southwestern Ohio.

**By Author Members of
Western Ohio Writers Association
(WOWA)**

*To Tracy,
My dear friend and beta
reader extraordinaire.*

*LD Masterson
aka Linda*

HANDCAR PRESS

flights of fiction

Copyright © 2013 by Michael Martin, Dennis L. Hitzeman, Tammy Newsom, Arch Little II, Lynda Sappington, Philip A. Lee, Liz Coley, Deanna Newsom, Kate Seegraves, LD Masterson, Bill Bicknell.

Executive Editor Gery L. Deer
Cover Design © 2012 by Michael Martin

www.handcarpress.com

First Handcar Press edition: April, 2013

ISBN 978-0-9885289-4-9 (Trade Paperback)

Western Ohio Writers Association Editorial Committee

Gery L. Deer, Executive Editor
Director/Co-Founder WOWA

Barbara A. Huiner-Deer
Co-Founder WOWA

Michael Martin
Kate Seegraves
Bill Bicknell
Philip A. Lee

Western Ohio Writers Association is a trademark of and an entertainment and educational arm of GLD Enterprises Commercial Writing.
www.westernohiowriters.org

Published in cooperation with GLD Enterprises Commercial Writing
PO Box 104, Jamestown, OH 45335
Ph: 937-902-4857
www.theconciergecopywriter.com

Table of Contents

INTRODUCTION

A LABOR OF LOVE

By Gery L. Deer

Executive Editor
Co-Founder, Director
Western Ohio Writers Association

D id you ever wonder what would happen if a group of authors got together for the sole purpose of ripping each other to shreds, leaving in their wake the mangled hopes, dreams, and tears of promising scribes who lay finally broken and decaying on the floor robbed of all dignity? Yeah, so did I!

So, in 2008, my wife Barbara and I decided to start a critique group for writers. But, we wanted something different than the usual "writers support group," where people just pat each other on the back and do their best not to upset anyone. I am a professional freelance commercial writer and journalist and I was used to people telling me when something was crap. If it was bad, I didn't get paid, and the rest of the writing industry works the same way. If we were going to be successful in our creative endeavors, we needed a group that didn't mind going for the jugular—be careful what you wish for.

Our goal for the Western Ohio Writers Association is to provide critique sessions, networking opportunities, and educational resources for writers in southwestern Ohio, northeastern Kentucky and southeastern Indiana. We meet monthly, with special public events such as the popular Beatnik Café live reading events held a few times a year. At first, there were only three of us, but soon the group expanded, and as of August, 2012, it includes some 100-plus participants on the website's membership list.

The critique sessions at the WOWA are not for the faint of heart, however. We're brutally honest, while kindly offering support and suggestions. We have a mixture of members from working writers and editors to those who just want to dabble in their favorite type of poetry or flash fiction.

The book you are about to read comes directly from those members with stories set in and around southwestern Ohio in areas near Dayton, Cincinnati and Columbus. Every story is an original work by the author, each of whom has a bio in the back of the book, in case you're interested in learning more about them.

Incidentally, if you think I'm kidding about how tough the critique can be in our group, you may take note that, although I started the WOWA, arranged for the publication of this book, provide meeting space, publicity and resources, and run the events, I am not listed among the contributing authors of this anthology. Nope. They threw me out of my own book. My story just wasn't good enough. Oh well, if you can't handle rejection, you might want to stay out of the writing business.

Although the editorial committee had a good snicker at my exclusion, fortunately for you, the discerning reader, they managed to find some great stories and we sincerely hope you'll enjoy them. And now sit back and relax as the Western Ohio Writers Association presents *FLIGHTS OF FICTION*.

THE DEAD OF WINTER

by Michael Martin

What I'm going to tell you only makes sense if you believe that I love my wife. If you can understand that—understand what it really means to love someone, stick with them through anything—then you'll forgo judging me. Wormwood salted the earth and smeared the sky with its dark Dust, and I see things pretty starkly now. But screw your judgment. I don't need it.

Miranda's huddled against me, cold as usual. It's been winter for seven bone-splintering months now, so I can't blame her. Ice and hunger make a soul cold, and it takes something warm and weighty to grab even a little heat back. She's bundled as best as can be managed, as am I. The low bunker wall, with snow and ice packed in front of it, cuts the wind some, but the cold relentlessly soaks in, regardless of shelter or layers.

I try to keep warm for both of us in the weak sunlight. Our home, a solid, brick farmhouse halfway between Dayton and Eaton, is big enough to offer some decent hiding places, but we can't afford to be cornered in it when they come. And they're coming. Perimeter alarms—taken from Bill's Hardware in New Lebanon and installed months ago a full mile away from the farmhouse—went off three minutes ago, which means we have five or ten, if we're lucky, before they're within shooting range. And it's not my intention to let anyone, human or worse, to get any closer than 50 feet. Just close enough to Peckinpah their trespassing keesters to kingdom come.

Course, that's only if I have to use the Nitro Mag tactical. The shotgun's three inch shells will pretty much puree anything in its range. But the Woodsmaster comes first. Not as messy as the Nitro, especially if I can hit the heart, or drill them through the eye. I use a scope—sue me. Maybe it's considered cheating if you're hunting *deer*. The two .357 Magnums holstered on my hips are for last stands, or in case any Dusted elephants come calling.

Don't laugh. The shit I've seen . . . well, transmogrified elephants would be right in line.

I look at Miranda, and a cold wholly different from the chill threatens to popsicle my blood as we wait. Thin and miserable, she crouches next to me, gripping herself and rocking back and forth. Once in a while, I get a glimpse of the girl who dragged me to the Kennedy Middle School Sadie Hawkins dance. A slight softening of her eyes, a loosening of her tense, stiff frame. But mostly, she shivers and moans.

Hell, *I'm* different. Harder, by necessity. Sentiment's a luxury I don't have the coin for, except when it comes to Miranda. But when I look at her, I mostly just see how I've . . . adjusted to things. Not how I wanted the last half of our lives to be, I can tell you.

Hunkered down here in the snow, freezing my fifty-four-year-old ass off, I'm in no mood to be judged. So if you're planning on categorizing my moral fiber, you're welcome to hop over the bunker wall and wait for your compadres, they of no scruples and merciless need. Miranda and I will paint the snow with your guts, and sleep better at night for it.

"Hang on, Miri," I say to her, shifting my feet and peering quickly over the bunker. She shivers some more and nudges against me. I don't see anything, and duck back down.

Even I acknowledge everything's different now, though. Maybe that's a good argument for walking away from what I promised her, promised God—and here's a big middle finger to the Heavenly Arbiter, if He even exists—promised in front of all our family and friends. Maybe the changed world means all bets are off, all vows so much tissue paper down a mean, swirling crapper. The end of the world would seem like a pretty good excuse to say, "Fuck it all. I'm taking care of me. You can go rot." But I don't care. She's my wife, and I meant what I vowed.

Of course, Wormwood doesn't argue. The ruin of all human life voiced its only opinion when it punched a hole in the earth's crust and showered the whole world with its infection.

Wormwood. I don't know who first called it that, but it surely sounds fitting. God promised never to give the planet another enema, so maybe that fiery piece of shit from the sky was His idea of a joke. "See," He says, "no water. Life preservers optional this time, folks." And, given how His Book says things will end, the name seemed right. Even if most of His followers aren't coherent—or alive— enough to appreciate the joke.

When it first struck, the damage was minimal, given what Wormwood could have done. It hit in the middle of the desert, so there weren't even any decent tsunamis from it. A few farmers and cattle incinerated, the lucky bastards. Men and cows probably all died with the same rounded O of shock and wonder on their faces, just before dandelioning into so many million atoms of powder and flame. The shockwave and firestorm sandpapered and fried a few more, but given that the rock wasn't all that big to begin with—just a few klicks wide—the bitch's opening salvo was pretty tame. Nope, she saved her big guns for the light show.

Seems as if ole Wormwood hit the perfect spot: not only did she throw up quite the mushroom cloud chock full of bugfuck molecules and germs, she hit a weak seam in crust. The resulting hole allowed magma from below to firehose out, created a supervolcano that simply added a few thousand shit-tons of pulverized crust into the atmosphere. Ordinarily, a lot of folks from these parts would be grooming small plots of carrots and tomatoes and corn to sell at the Webster Street Market in Dayton. Thanks to Wormwood, we're instead luxuriating in the wonderful June weather of today: eight or ten inches of powder on the ground, with more sure to come before the fall and winter arrive and really show us who's boss.

The magic combination of raw planetary fire and rock and

Wormwood's own mysterious components mixed and wrapped near the entire world in its dusky grip. Stained the sky first, then sifted down, and sprinkled us all like rain of toxic pixie dust.

Wormwood's makeup and aim have caused a lot of loony speculating, as you might imagine. A hefty amount of the survivors I've met seem to have nothing better to do but spin tales of government conspiracies, demonic pacts and Central American myths. Not me. Wondering's all good, but it doesn't put meat on the table, and it doesn't keep the Dusted from eating you, or all-too-human looters from killing you, taking your gun and *then* maybe eating you if nothing else is handy.

Yeah, the Dusted. It's what we've taken to calling the humans and animals changed by Wormwood's witch's brew. Which is most everyone, from what I can tell, excepting a tiny fraction of people. A good number of animal species are susceptible, too—maybe two-thirds? Three quarters? It's not like anyone's had the time to take a census. And no one knows why some aren't changed. At least not yet. If any scientists have survived, I suppose there's a slim thread of hope that they might find out why. Not that it'll do the few billion ruined lives any good.

If you're one of the unlucky ones, just a little of the Dust will do. There's really no telling how you'll end up, though humans seem the least changed by it—on the outside, at least. I've seen coyotes with hides like armadillos and double-hinged jaws fill will rows of shark teeth. I've seen possums with bat wings and three eyes. I won't even *talk* about what Dust does to squirrels. Humans, though . . . there are some visible changes, but most of the changing is inside. Dusted people are ravenous cannibals, unable to survive on anything but human flesh. Somewhere, George Romero is laughing his ass off. Or getting his face eaten by his neighbors.

Miranda cries thinly and points back toward the house. Swearing, I grab the shotgun and peer against the bright snow. I didn't expect them to come from behind us.

Something is crossing the brief, cold expanse between the house and bunker, but it isn't human. I can't afford to stand up—the imminent marauders would surely see me, blowing our advantage of surprise—so I brace myself as well as I can against the bunker wall and sight along both barrels. The dark thing does this stomach-churning half crawl, half leap towards us, and makes a sound like a baby being stuck with rusty forks.

Guts curdling, I realize it's a cat. A cat with three black tentacles pulling itself towards us, a ghastly green light in its eyes, glowing even in daylight.

Fucking cats. Dogs proved immune to Dust, but cats turned out to be extremely susceptible. I hadn't heard of a single case where a cat wasn't turned into a cross of Dante and Giger.

Gritting my teeth, I follow the furred abomination as it sploshes across the snow towards us. It gathers itself for one big, wet leap–and I spray it with buckshot. Just as it detonates across the snow in a hail of black and green, there's a nanosecond when I think I hear an actual meow.

I feel a quick pang of loss for Ranger; best dog a man could have. Ranger could have taken the Dusted cat and let us keep focused on the human threat. Despite being immune, he still turned mean after the Dust fell. It's a bad day when a man has to choose between his dog and his wife, but Ranger bit Miranda twice. And I take my vows seriously. But if other men chose differently, I can't say I blame them. Not all wives are Miranda.

Miranda. I turn to check on her, and she's staring at the dark splotch in the snow, an unreadable look on her cold-pinched face. Despite the danger, despite the changes Wormwood has wrought on our lives, for a moment I see her at sixteen. Long auburn hair, brown eyes warmer than the best mug of coffee, and a smile that was equal parts mischief, mystery, and affection.

Then I hear a howling from the other direction. A distinctively human sound, this time, a murderous variant of the old rebel yell. No octopod cats or rhino-sized wolves this time. They're here, and they're not going to be satisfied with anything less than our deaths.

"Stay low, Miri, until I say so. Close your eyes if you have to." Dropping the shotgun, I pick up the sniper rifle and sight over the top of the camouflaged bunker.

Four of them emerge from the tree line. Squinting against the snow glare and sun, I see only one with a gun—looks like a pistol. The others hold machetes or axes. About a football field away. They're running, but with a determined purpose. I think about shouting out an offer to share or give food, but one glance at Miranda kills that idea. Past experience has shown me that human marauders can be as bad as Dusted ones.

I breathe slowly and evenly, let go of the sickness roiling in my guts, look down the scope. They're running straight at me. Morons. Even Dusted manage to crazily zigzag when careening along. Assholes probably drive a truck with a Confederate flag window sticker, too. Squinting at the crosshairs, I squeeze the trigger. The one with a gun takes few steps before he realizes he's dead, a dark red flower blooming across his chest.

The others, hearing the shot and spotting me, scream in fury and sprint towards me, snow flying in their wake. Sliding another round home, I close one eye, put another chest in the crosshairs, and fire. He—no, she, dammit, a woman—lets out a strangled bark and flips backward into the snow, twitching and bleeding. Two more, but they're less than twenty meters away.

Miranda looks like she's trying to sink into the stone of the bunker as I drop the rifle and yank out the .357s. I'd prefer the shotgun, but need the extra bullets just in case. The high from fear and adrenaline can make them harder to kill than junkies jumped up with PCP. If I miss, I don't want to stop to reload.

As I turn back toward them, I see them peel away from each other, heading toward either end of the bunker. A spike of fear as I realize Miranda is closer to her end of the bunker than I am to mine.

Abruptly, crazily, I remember the first time I held her at that dance, all the wonderfully perilous curves of her body brushing against my arms. Blinking, I hear a loud sound, realize I'm shouting back at the looters. Holding a pistol in each hand, I unload four quick shots into the center of the axe-wielding woman running at me, her mouth stretched in a feral shout of her own. Without waiting for her to drop, I spin, snow whirling around my feet and run towards the last attacker. No, *no*. I see his arm above Miranda, rusty blade about to split her skull. Gritting my teeth, I empty the clip into his head. He drops jerkily, splashing blood and brains across the bunker, the snow, and Miranda. "I LOVE MY WIFE, DAMN YOU!" I scream at the twitching corpse. Relief and nausea tumble like coked up dervishes in my guts.

Trembling, I drop to my knees. The only sound is Miranda's breathing, now steady and even. Tears wet my cheeks, and I know they'll freeze soon if I don't get warm. But I can't move. The gun is hot in my hand, but any burns I receive are deserved: my own customized marks of Cain, tattooed into my flesh for the sins I've committed for love.

A hesitant shadow blocks the sun, and a soft touch pulls my attention up from the corrupted snow. I look up at Miranda, and I recognize the gleam in her eyes. I struggle to my feet, gather the weapons, and begin reloading. Without looking at her, I nod sharply. I hear her leap over the bunker, towards the farthest fallen body.

I try to block the sounds of her feeding, and wish I could go inside. But there might be more coming. I love my wife, you see. I won't let them have her.

ST. GEORGE AND THE DRAGON

by Dennis L. Hitzeman

I sat at the counter facing the street, nursing my coffee and considering the morning. In most cities, I find the best breakfasts at what some would consider to be the most questionable establishments.

They're usually dives in downtowns, packed then deserted by successive waves of suited and briefcased workers indulging in the pleasure of a blue collar meal before trudging off to their stifling cubicles for the day. They're also a good place to think and to watch people, to learn a little about the place I happen to be, and only rarely does anyone ask why I am there.

Ned's was one of those places; the size of a closet with the only seating being a single counter along the plate-glass window facing the street. Ned's was my kind of place, if such a place actually existed.

My reasons for being at Ned's that morning were dubious at best, even for someone in my line of work. The problem is that my employer pays me a lot to find people. I usually don't know why, and I usually don't care. This time, I suspected I did, and that knowledge left me more uncomfortable than I had ever been about a job.

Thinking about the job returned my attention to the note now crumpled beyond recognition in my left hand. Their instructions had been curt and beyond misinterpretation. I had a lead and I had to follow it, even if it turned into nothing. It was the promise of finding something worth pursuing that made me keep trying.

"I killed that, you know."

The grizzled old man sitting on the next stool startled me out of my revelry, and I almost asked him what he was talking about. Instead, he nodded toward the sculpture that dominated the boulevard outside.

It was a gleaming stainless steel monstrosity catching the morning sun, a series of horizontal I-beams extending from a sinuous central spine mounted high on posts so that it hovered over a city block. It did look kind of like the remains of some long dead, massive beast, at least to the more imaginative. According to the plaque mounted in the little park at one end, it was supposed to celebrate the first powered flight.

"I'm not sure I understand," I said, then retreated to my coffee. I hoped he wouldn't press the issue. I wasn't in the mood yet, especially not today. The man, on the other hand, seemed like he was in the mood to share.

He shook his head. "No one remembers anything anymore."

I sighed because I figured I was not going to get out of the conversation he wanted to have. Besides, I'm a sucker for a good story. That was one of the reasons I found myself eating a greasy spoon breakfast despite my misgivings about the task at hand.

I glanced at him sidelong as he scowled at the sculpture with the gaze of a warrior sizing up an opponent. He seemed like he was carved out of an old piece of driftwood and hung with clothes that might have been in fashion when that first flight occurred. His weathered face seemed to glow with the wisdom of age and the outdoors.

I took him to be homeless.

"The plaque says it's a sculpture about the first flight or something."

He waved his hand. "That's what they all say . . ."

Then he shook his head and shrugged his shoulders. His face showed a sadness that seemed to echo through his whole body. It was almost as if I could feel his emotion like the coffee cup gripped in my right hand.

"What's the truth?" I said.

His voice was a hoarse whisper, as if he was sharing his dying wish with me.

"The truth is that I slew a dragon once and saved all these damned people from slavery and fiery death," he said.

"A dragon?" I nearly choked on my coffee and felt terrible about it, though I could never have told him why. The paper in my left hand suddenly felt like a heavy weight. Or a stick of dynamite ready to explode.

Now, he glanced sidelong at me. "Yeah, a dragon. What do you think them boys wanted to build a flying machine for anyway?"

I turned toward him, and his gaze caught mine like a vise. I noticed a faded scar that traced his jaw from his chin to his ear beneath his three-day stubble. His face reminded me of pictures my grandfather had shown me of his buddies during the last world war. His eyes were what made me look away, though. They were like the hard steel of the sculpture reflecting the sun.

"Seems hard to believe that no one would remember a dragon, dead or alive," I said.

The man grunted. "It's easy to forget what you don't want to remember. Nobody remembers that Jesus died for their sins neither. Besides, man's always wanted to fly because the enemy flies too."

Great, a religious fanatic and nuts, I thought. Somehow, such things always seemed to go hand in hand. His expression told me he believed every word of it, though, and somewhere in the back of my head a voice said I should too.

"Well, not everybody believes that kind of stuff," I said.

"I don't suppose you do either," he said.

I didn't want to start a religious debate, but I'd never had an opportunity like the one in front of me in all my years of work.

"I don't believe I know your name," I said.

Now the man laughed. "You won't believe my name either."

"Try me."

"George Nicomedias the Seventy-fifth," he said.

"The seventy-fifth?"

"Yeah, my kind's been around for a long time." He didn't even bat an eye. He had a good imagination, if nothing else.

"Well, George, at least let me buy your coffee," I said.

He shook his head, "I couldn't let you do that."

"Why not?"

He cast a glance at my left hand, and I couldn't help but shudder.

"You look like you work for a living and times are tough," he said. "I've had more than my fair share, and I can't take what I have now with me. Only seems fair that I pay."

He stepped down from the stool and turned toward me. "Besides, you didn't head for the street when I started telling stories. That means more to me than you could know."

He clasped my hand quickly, pressing something heavy and hard into it.

"Put his breakfast and my coffee on my tab, Ned," he said to the man through the order window behind us.

"Sure thing, George," the cook said.

Then George turned on his heel and in a few steps was out the door and on his way down the street. I knew I should go after him, but my feet were rooted in place.

In my hand was a coin whose origin and age I could only guess. I had no doubt it was gold. One side was stamped with a man's head and something in Latin. On the other was a man on horseback killing a dragon. My heart skipped a beat.

"That George is something else," Ned said from the window.

"He seems to be," I said.

It was always best not to know what the business was about, I always said. My employer paid me to find people, not to care. But now, for the first time in my life, I looked out at the sculpture in the street and started to wonder about dragons.

DEAR MR. CHANEY

by Tammy Newsom

It was nightfall. The last daily stop on the Miamisville Traction Line ended at the covered bridge in Germantown. The yellow harvest moon faced Twin Creek as the fog curled up in thick tendrils. On this night, there were two riders left standing at the traction car drop-off: the car operator and a costumed ghoul riding the car to town. The operator hated stopping here; it was such an isolated place. He wondered if the Headless Horseman would choose this route to Sleepy Hollow. This lone rider had to be the last of the revelers to arrive before tomorrow's Fall Festival's commencement activities, but he would not remove his disguise.

The passenger's hair was like two old brooms swept under a top hat; his jack-o'-lantern smile was fixed. The flesh itself seemed to peel away from the nose and cheekbones. Worse than the frozen smile, were the eyes, which were lidless and protruding. The driver surmised his features must be taped into place, but could see no tape or string. The passenger's face was a veritable death mask. The car operator dropped the ghoul's two satchels onto the inverted bowstring bridge, next to the platform, and backed away from the sliding doors.

The passenger tilted his fixed stare over his shoulder, then turned and lunged forward past the driver. Although his movements were oddly graceful, he deliberately scraped his left foot across the bridge's wooden planks to affect a limp. The operator shuddered and countered with a widened stance. The two of them circled each other until the ghoul exited the car. The operator then shouted at his back, "You can keep your pretzels!" and slammed the doors. The ghoul turned to face the vanishing car. "Rude," the traveler muttered. "Only having fun at you." He sniffed at the air for pretzels.

The scent of condensed sweet liquor and burnt smokestacks emanated from town. He hobbled towards it, sprightly, through the moonlight and fog; the eventual promise of a warm bed and stiff drink cut through the brisk autumn night. A few minutes later, he had nearly reached his destination, so he looked around for the closest streetlamp. With two clawed fingers, he delicately retrieved a worn letter from the inside coat pocket and inspected its address under the light. Was he sent on a fool's errand to rob some poor lady of her family secrets? Perhaps.

Let me appeal to her imagination. he had told them.

Why was this so important that you go? They asked. *We have people to handle this. This could easily turn to another* Nosferatu. *You don't want to get your hands dirty.*

It's the hands-on that entreats me, he said.

Bauer Opera House on South Main was only a ten minute walk from the trolley stop. Its façade was discreet; it contained one stained glass portal at the top of a single door—not nearly as grand as the Victoria, whose marbled walls were covered in some of the finest area murals. Across the street from Bauer was Laff's Tavern. The man could hear laughter steeped by rum. He followed their inebriated conversations for a moment before he reached for the opera house's iron knocker. A few guffaws and loud voices indicated that someone had knocked over a bucket of ice cold water reserved for apple bobbing.

Meanwhile, a block away on Center Street, two young boys were finishing up a night game of stickball. Despite the chill, the children were perspiring in their bare feet. They hopped between shadows, to avoid the moonlight. At once, they saw an unfamiliar silhouette vamp up the brick sidewalk towards their house. The boys then grabbed their sticks and tip toed stealthily to where he stood. Their temples pulsed with blood, and fear tuned their senses to a heightened pitch. He heard their bare feet patter behind him.

"Ha-ha, "the interloper cried gleefully, and hissed. Filed, pointed teeth protruded from his crooked mouth. He raised his arms high above his head and grandly flourished his cape like bat wings. His body lowered into an extended plié stance. "No!" "Monster!" they screamed. They raised their bats and swung, prepared to smash the fiend's skull like a pumpkin. The man screamed and knelt to his knees, "No, no, not the fashe!"

Upstairs, Opera House owner and sole proprietor, Mayeva Nicolai, was dozing in front of the living room fire when she was awakened by knocks at the front door interspersed with several shrill screams. Was it a wolf howling, or a dog? She marshaled the silver handled cane, which belonged to her late husband, and skipped down the three flights of marble stairs to the lighted street below. A few people from the Tavern had ceased their festivities to gather outside; some of them carried their glasses with them, and watched the assault with unaffected interest. They weren't sure what they were seeing.

Mayeva first noticed two duffle bags discarded next to the man's body, while the boys organized their assault. Ari, the older, had concentrated kicking his side with his knee, while Bela, the younger, swung a stickball bat at his head. The magician-ghoul swam and rolled his body on the front sidewalk. He managed to deflect most of their blows with an extended arm, but lost his top hat in the fray. His wig and hat had rolled into the patch of moonlight, and he reached a wavering hand for the door.

"No." he said. "It's jush me . . . don' ship on a shpider . . ."

Mayeva's face twisted from terror, to relief and recognition. "Darlings, stop," she commanded. She stamped her cane to the ground, which broke their concentration immediately. The boys' motion ceased and turned their attention to the silver tipped cane their mother bore. "Yes, mother," they demurred.

She waved for her neighbors, who had just started to get interested, to go back inside the building. She rushed to her boys' side and held them motionless. Her boys were seven and nine years old— getting stronger and more difficult to control by the day. This may set a bad precedent for them.

"You are both very brave," she assuaged them, quietly enough to stay out of the spectators' earshot. "But this is Mr. Chaney. He is our friend. You know, The Man of 1000 Faces. 'Don't–step-on-a-Spider. It–may-be–Lon-Chaney.' I told you he might be coming. Now, apologize to Mr. Chaney. You both lost control tonight. You need to come in now and wash up for bed."

"Oh-h-h. Momma, it's the Phantom!"

"No," her younger son cried, "It's the Hunchback!"

"He doesn't have a hump!" Ari corrected his brother.

The boys stood motionless, watching him keenly. Chaney's sagebrush of hair had fallen to the side to reveal perfectly a greased and combed black coif underneath. One of his wire loops, which he had used in several films to make his eyes bulge, had dropped out. One eye was free to close completely, while the other eye remained propped open.

"Ouch. Don't shep on a shpider." Chaney's elastic features twisted in and out of shape, while he jumped lithely to his feet. He held out a talon to inspect his eye. Forgetting about the five inch long nails glued to his fingers, he inadvertently scratched the cornea. Chaney let out a fresh yelp.

"Are you okay?" Mayeva asked. Chaney nodded, covered his eye.

"Only a few bruishish. They didn't hit me that hard."

"Well, now you know you shouldn't scare the children like that. You could get yourself killed." Both boys remained motionless. They had not moved since their mother told them to stop, and their breathing slowed as they watched him stand to his feet.

"Of courssh, Madam," Chaney brushed himself off, retrieved his hat, and beamed the boys a one-eyed glare. "My apologiesh. I wash going to surprissh *you all*, but then the children were already there . . . you know-I-I-don't like my public to shee me without my makeup." He turned to the last spectator from Laff's and called out facetiously, "Thanksh. Thanksh for all you help."

Mayeva called to the spectator, who looked confused, "I am trying out a new fortune teller for my booth, tomorrow! If he is good, you'll see him there!"

They smiled and waved, oblivious of the star's identity, then turned back inside for another drink.

"*If* I'm good?"

Marina bent closer to look at him, her demeanor more maternal than star-struck.

"Poor dumb beast. Let me see your eye."

"No, no," he flinched and jerked away. "It hurtsh."

"Don't be a baby." She moved again to him slower and gently lifted the eye lid to inspect the afflicted orb, and clicked her tongue. He sucked in some air and flinched again. She couldn't be too angry at him, although luckily his eye was not too badly scratched. Ari started to whimper.

"Go inside, now boys. He's okay." They mustn't raise attention.

Ari looked at his brother and asked, "Is Mr. Chaney going to read our fortunes?" Bela shrugged. They disappeared inside, presumably to go upstairs to their room.

"Mr. Chaney, please, will you allow me to remove the wire loop off your other eye socket to avoid injury to that one, too? The sight of them both is turning my stomach." Chaney shrank his shoulders, defeated, at giving away his identity. Mayeva gingerly removed the wire loop from around the non injured eye, and Chaney automatically blinked, pleased at the release of pressure.

"Thanks. I have been wearing thosh wire loopshinsh Dayton. You have any eye dropsh at home?"

"I have something that will do . . . an old gypsy remedy, "she motioned him to move behind her. "Please, upstairs, I can treat you eye there."

Chaney nodded and pointed to the Tavern. "You lied to thosh people."

"Yes. Can we talk inside?" She hurried him through the door and closed it behind them. "Neither of us needs the scrutiny of prying neighbors. You, because you're likely to be mobbed. And us, because we don't want any trouble."

"No harm done." Chaney smoothed out his frock and trousers, and straightened the floppy bow on his necktie.

"How did you recognishe me in makeup?"

"We are very devoted fans of the Man of 1000 Faces. This is the same makeup you wore in *London after Midnight*. Very cute. Were you going to hypnotize me, doctor?"

Mayeva, a diminutive woman, struggled to assist him up the two flights of stairs. Although she leveraged the cane for support, she still managed to slam them both into the wall several times on the way. Once they reached the second floor, she stopped in front of her apartment, where she considered arranging him in front of the warm fireplace, with a cup of simmering hot tea. She could hear water running in the bathroom, drowning out her sons' excited voices.

She paused, and changed her mind. She decided she couldn't pass up an opportunity.

"Mr. Chaney, I know you might not be feeling so well, but may I walk you upstairs to show you my opera stage?" She motioned with her head. "I-I just don't know when you might be returning to visit our little showstopper. I know you're a thespian at heart," she explained. She supported him through one last flight of stairs, as he grew steadier on his feet.

Chaney nodded, "I can walk myshelf thanksh. What a darling little shage company thisish." Chaney patted her arm and shrugged off her shoulder, asserting that he could walk unassisted the rest of the way.

Chaney peeked around the hallway and into the Opera Hall; the ceiling was no more than twenty feet high. "People shing in here? Where's the orcheshruh pit?" he chided. "Is thish a danshtodio?"

"Not to be critical, Mr. Chaney, but if you ever do talking pictures, you're going to have to build better vampire teeth." He blinked his eyes a few more times, and then peeled off his set of fingernails and fangs, which tended to poke through his lips. He repeated his questions, unencumbered.

Mayeva laughed. "No place here for people to sing? This, from a man who made a *silent* picture about Opera? Your *Phantom* would make a much better troupe musical."

Chaney licked at the sticky gum residue on his teeth. "It was a love story between beauty and the beast. If she hadn't had the audacity to remove his mask, she would have stayed with him forever."

She chuckled at him and continued with the tour. He quietly vowed to himself that he would interject his own baritone in a talkie remake of the film, as he was about to do with *The Unholy Three.*

"Our Opera House is a multi functional space, Mr. Chaney. Germantown uses this as a Town Hall, and community gathering place. Also, a Concert Hall and a central medium for all local performance venues."

The third floor Opera Hall had six tall windows facing the street, with an octagonal proscenium surrounded intimately with 360-degree audience seating. This was a traditional theatre in the round set up. Across the hall were adjoining offices, which had often doubled for dressing rooms. During performances, Mayeva told him, the musicians were expected to either mingle with the audience or prop themselves next to the players.

Shop patrons were used to the noise created during live performances, but her husband had installed rolled fiber over the dressing room walls to block out the late night rehearsals. Chaney nodded in appreciation at the resourcefulness of such a dedicated theatrical family.

***

"Your children don't seem to mind late nights."

"Yes, I am really sorry about that, Mr. Chaney. They are really very good boys, but they are also protective of me, now, since it's just the three of us."

With the tour ended, Mayeva asked, "I see you didn't arrive with an entourage. That is what I had expected," she breathed. "Will you use a pseudonym to check into the Florentine?" Chaney blinked a few more times before he answered.

"Max Shrek," He improvised, blotting his chin. Noticing blood on his fingers, he realized he must have bitten through his lip.

"The German actor, who played the vampire in *Nosferatu*?" she asked.

Chaney shrugged, "*Nosferatu* was a better picture than *London after Midnight.*"

"And a financial disaster," she broke in. "Bram Stoker's widow sued for copyright infringement. Nobody made a dime."

"Only because she didn't want her husband's work exploited by greedy sideshow freaks, like me," Chaney answered, and thumped his chest.

"Mm." She stopped and scanned him for a moment, listened, and then told him, "Wait here." She disappeared to the bedrooms in the back of the apartment to check on her two boys. Chaney tried to make out the conversation, but could only glean fragments of their interaction at the door.

". . . Maybe tomorrow . . . Mr. Chaney . . . Autograph when he comes back . . . some excitement . . ." Chaney could hear the bedsprings creak. He imagined they must have climbed into bed, pulled the covers up to their chins, squeezed their eyes shut, and dreamed they caught Santa in the act of delivering toys.

Mayeva returned to the living room, where Chaney was waiting, with a small jar of ointment. He had settled quite comfortably into one of the high backs next to the fireplace, his hat and coat draped over the chair. He observed that the apartment's white painted brick walls were covered in movie stills and promotional posters, alongside Turkish décor: heavy curtains, ceramic jars, and colorful beads.

"What is that for?" he asked, looking at the jar she carried.

"Your eye. If you hope to not see it infected."

"What's in that?"

Mayeva answered, "Old gypsy remedy, remember?

"Ah," Chaney chuckled.

It was Mayeva's turn to smile. "Iodine and sulfuric acid."

Chaney gasped. "What?"

"I'm fooling you. This isn't really a gypsy remedy, "she quipped. He had started to relax again, until he smelled the sulfuric iodide she blotted into the corner of his eye. He jerked, prepared to howl in pain, but stopped at how salving the concoction was to the affected area.

"This ointment is remarkable."

"Yes. Don't touch it." Mayeva blocked his hand from rubbing his eye. She folded a gauze patch over his eye and attempted to tape it closed. He brushed her hand away.

"The eye will heal itself in a few days if you keep it covered," she reprimanded him.

"Later. I need to see where I'm going first, though. Thank you." He stuffed the gauze and tape in his pocket. How else would he read her facial expressions when he questioned her?

She assented and returned the jar and medical supplies to the kitchen cupboard, feeling both guilty and slightly affronted.

Chaney called, "I did my research on you, Mrs. Nicolai. The Census Bureau named you as one of the region's registered Romani." His eye, although blurry where the topical solution had obscured his vision, was completely free of pain.

Mayeva returned and sat down in the chair opposite Chaney, next to the fireplace. "Well, my Vardo is parked next to my husband's Model T."

"And the fact that you owned an opera house . . . I had to meet you."

"Thank you, Mr. Chaney, "said Mayeva. "I'm flattered. Yes, you mentioned in your letter that you require my particular expertise for research into a film venture. That last film of yours—a murdering circus performer who cuts off both of his arms to win the heart of his love interest—was deeply disturbing." She shook her head.

"Although your passion moved me, Joan Crawford wasn't worth it."

"*The Unknown.* Well I can assure you, Madam, no woman will get such devotion from me."

She smiled. "Can you really smoke with your feet?" She handed him a drag, to be sure. Chaney pulled his lighter from the inside pocket and removed his socks and shoes to reveal a set of freakishly dexterous toes. He placed the drag in his mouth and lighter between his first two toes. He then held his foot flat against his chest, and bent his big toe back to ignite the flame. He reached down to inhale and puff, hands free.

"Marvelous!" she laughed and clapped, having forgotten to be quiet. She stopped and looked back towards the boys' room.

"Maybe the kids would like to see this trick tomorrow before I leave . . . if they trust me enough," he said.

"Of course," Mayeva said. She hoped her next remark wasn't too blunt for the star. "Maybe. Mm. Like the rest of your devoted public, Mr. Chaney, I heard the rumors of what brought you to the new film industry. You quit the vaudeville circuit and sought a divorce on account of your former wife's suicide attempt."

His great piercing eyes, known for their complexity and emotional depth, widened and refocused like a camera lens letting in light. He hunched over his foot, curled his toes tighter around the cigarette, and took another drag. He realized he would have to give her something, in order to get back.

"Yes, that's right," he said. "That's what led me to go into pictures. Cleva attempted suicide by swallowing a bottle of mercury in the wings during one of my performances in Oklahoma City. She thought I was cheating on her with one of the chorus girls."

"Oh, how awful."

"That little jealous stunt cost us both our stage careers, and she, her lovely singing voice. We were both blackballed from the industry. Although, she also did me a favor. I realized that my marriage, much like vaudeville, was dead."

"And then?"

"I married my darling Hazel, took custody of Creighton, and moved my family to Hollywood. "

"What does your son do, Mr. Chaney?"

"Creighton is in business school. He will *never* go into show business, while I'm alive."

"And now?"

"Another change is imminent. You were right about *Phantom of the Opera*. The sound revolution is here, Mrs. Nicolai," he said. "And I want to get on board with my particular brand of pathos. I think audiences will eat it up. Characters based on, or, invoking the, uh, superstitions of your people: vampires, werewolves, mummies, and even Shelley's opiate-induced *Frankenstein*."

"The superstitions of my people?"

"You and your husband's people. The gypsies."

"You mean the Romany," she corrected him.

Chaney put on his socks and shoes, and waited for her to ask the next question.

She asked, "So, how am I supposed to help you accomplish this sound revolution of yours?"

"Well," Chaney said, "as I mentioned in my letter, Tod Browning, the famed MGM producer and I, are researching some plot ideas for Universal Pictures. They are preparing a series of new talking films to meet the demands of the burgeoning horror market. Only on a much larger scale than what has been done before. The first project will feature me in the title role of Bram Stoker's masterpiece."

She rose from her high back and returned to the kitchen to prepare an ice pack. "Are you doing research or are you checking for fan loyalty before committing to any costly projects?"

"Well, we also want to do a werewolf picture, but we don't have a script yet."

The fire was still blazing and Chaney closed his eyes, dabbling at the blood on his mouth. Mayeva stood up from her chair, and then returned with ice chips wrapped in a towel. She held it to his face. He decided to try another tactic.

"You'd make a wonderful nurse," he said, holding the ice pack to his mouth. "I didn't mean to offend you."

"Thank you. I am not offended," she answered, having returned to her seat. "I am just correcting a common mistake. I run a struggling theatre, sir. I am a widow with two strapping boys, as you have observed. Honestly, I don't envy you. And I wonder if you, yourself, don't miss those days, Mr. Chaney, when you had the freedom and anonymity to connect directly with the audience? I just don't understand why you couldn't consult with your Hollywood types before traveling all the way out to Germantown, Ohio to get a stick in your eye."

Chaney nodded. "That's why I'm here, to connect with you, my audience." He laid his hand over his heart. He continued, "I could pull some strings, you know. Get you a job in Hollywood, as a stage manager, or a producer, perhaps. Maybe even as an artistic consultant. Wouldn't that make things easier for you and the boys, financially? "

"No. This is our home. My husband I and moved here years ago as a young couple. I bring art, singing and storytelling to this community. My sons have friends; they go to school on the hill. This may be a small village, but people accept us here. We offer them a much valued service. That's the problem with you rich movie stars: you think people can be bought."

Mayeva had hoped to discourage him. Chaney smiled. He knew she wanted to understand his intentions first. "Well this is your chance, isn't it Mrs. Nicolai. To set the record straight. To tell the public how it really began. Where do the legends come from? I assure you, I will bring nothing but artistic integrity to the record. No tricks, no sleight of hand."

"Audiences don't want the truth, Mr. Chaney. They want to be entertained. Aren't you aware of this? This 'research' of yours will never see the light of day because Hollywood will twist it to their liking just to sell tickets," She added, "I am afraid you are a cursed man, Mr. Chaney, plundering the Pharaoh's tomb."

"How so?"

"The dead never leave us; they grow in number as we weave a tapestry of family history. Spirits, regardless of whether they are good or evil, may not respond favorably to our ancient family secrets exploited to a gnawing public. I fear you may be the sacrificial lamb."

Chaney suppressed a snicker. "Yes, and we all know about Santa, the Jolly Old Elf."

"Mr. Chaney, you shouldn't have come. I am neither witch nor gypsy, but I have been called both. I don't want to see your career cut short. Hollywood is better off with you in it. Think of the hype surrounding *Dracula*. There are still no authorized versions of the story on film, and Bram Stoker is dead. His wife did not give Murnau her permission for the story rights, even after production. And although, Murnau never offered her a dime, she did this all on account of protection for the people involved—whether they deserved it or not."

Chaney studied her before answering. "You are keen to Hollywood gossip. With all due respect, Madam, you don't appear to realize that the book, *Dracula,* was based a nightmare of Stoker's. He just filled in the gaps using the story of Vlad the Impaler." He added, for clarification, "One of the most fiendish brutes in history—"

"A national hero to some of his subjects," Mayeva stopped him, and revealed a trace Romanian accent. She refused to be patronized. "Some of the best stories do come from dreams."

"But I don't have Stoker's inspiration. I need yours." Chaney cajoled. He closed his eyes and laid his head back in the chair. Chaney had learned to act through people watching, in order to perform skits for his deaf parents. He pulled the gauze patch out of his pocket and taped it over his eye. "Tell me, Mayeva. Tell me about the 'land of thieves and phantoms'."

Mayeva answered, "I really have nothing to benefit you in your movie enterprise. Just a sad oral tradition, passed down through my family, starting from the time Noah crashed his ark into the Turkish mountains."

"Your family line goes back to Noah?" Although both eyes were closed his face was rapt, as though watching a procession of images behind his painted lids.

"Only the cursed line."

"Please, go on."

"Humanity faces only two true dangers: those actions, which cause us to destroy others and those which cause us to destroy ourselves. However, even those with the purest of hearts—with the best of intentions—we are often subject to those forces beyond our control."

"You're saying?" Chaney asked, lost for a moment.

"People often do shocking things out of self preservation."

"Yes," he agreed. "We all know the road to hell is paved with good intentions." He added, "Especially in the fall."

"You read my poem . . ." she stopped.

Chaney opened his eyes and sighed, "I know your poem."

He recited: *"Even a man who is pure at heart—and says his prayers by night—can become a Wolf when the Wolf bane blooms and the Autumn Moon is bright . . ."*

She continued, her voice was coming from far away. ". . . Vampire and Lycanthrope have been around since creation, mutations I suppose. To be fair, their condition is only contagious to their relatives. I have a reason for wanting to remain here, anchored to this town. Society, as a whole, has lived in the dark for a very long time. We really believed we were protected by talismans and faith. Now we have new technological advancements to begin to climb again out of the dark: electricity, mobility, the freedom to live in peace."

Images of night creatures flooded Chaney's brain: timid, starving, and hiding in the Carpathians. Their numbers had been washed out less than a century after the Deluge. Fearing extinction, they only ventured out after dark under a bright moon. One of the brothers had cut a deal: protection in exchange for the occasional ritualistic sacrifice.

An hour later, Chaney left the apartment. He handed Mayeva his prop teeth and matted sheep's wool wig, "Let Bela and Ari have these, when they wake up tomorrow," he whispered with one last wink. "These are my special signature props. At your suggestion, I will have to devise teeth to better enunciate for listening audiences."

"Wonderful," she said. "Thank you."

He considered her diatribe before he spoke again. "You may might be right, Madam. We won't reproduce your story, exactly. But it will influence how we proceed."

Chaney flipped his hat to her, and left. Other than the one eye patch, his face was free of prosthetics and greasepaint. He checked into the Florentine on Market Street under the name, Max Shrek. The following day, he came back to entertain the boys at the Festival before flying home on the prestigious Trimotor. No one had recognized the identity of the one eyed juggler—not even when he handed the Nicolai boys all his quarter tips.

***

Ten months later, in August 1930, Hollywood observed an hour of silence to mourn the death of the father of monster makeup, Master of Horror, and Man of 1000 faces—Lon Chaney. As a tribute, production on all active film projects ceased during this hour.

Mayeva listened to the live radio broadcast of his funeral. Afterward, she turned off the sound, and then pulled a stepladder down the hall to climb eye level with her beloved *Phantom of the Opera* movie still. This still, released after the film's opening, had immortalized the moment when the Phantom's terrifying skull-like face was revealed to audiences for the first time. She climbed up and caressed the poster affectionately, before covering it with a black veil, fastened by clothespins.

"My dear Mr. Chaney, I won't forget you," she sobbed. "But now that you're gone, who will they get to play *Dracula?*" She climbed down the steps from the empty rehearsal hall space to the apartment rooms, below, to serve up a couple of bloody lamb steaks for dinner.

Bela seemed to favor the entrails.

A CHICK STORY

by Arch Little II

Bethany Louise pulled her fuel-efficient car over to the side of the road on Lakeshore Drive. The *thuckita thuckita* sound from the vehicle's flat tire was now too loud for her to ignore. Her kind, elderly father had always told her, "Louie Poo, you must check your tires every now and then with the gauge to stay out of trouble." However, when she went to use the tire gauge, she noticed that it had some kind of icky goo on it. Since she had not wanted to get any on her hands, she had decided to wait until her younger brother could check the tire for her. He was great with such things. However, now she felt like a total poopy head. It was too late to take her father's advice or get her brother's assistance. She was stuck on a dark, deserted back road in southern Ohio and even worse, she could hear a storm coming. She would just have to change the tire herself, which would most certainly involve some greasy tools or getting dirt under her fresh manicure. Louie Poo turned the volume to the Oprah radio station up so that she could hear the Michael Bolton marathon as she got out of her new hybrid SUV.

Bethany Louise (or "B Lo" as the janitor at her apartment building called her) kicked the tire as she verified that it was indeed flat. Cursing her misfortune, she was unsure how best to proceed. She walked around to the front of the car and lifted the hood to the engine compartment. Nervously curling a strand of her long blond hair in her fingers, Bethany wondered where the spare tire might be kept. Sliding her glove over her left hand, she twisted the cap to the radiator. Hopefully, a secret spare tire storage space might then reveal itself. She took a surprised step back when steam whooshed out instead.

Just then the music stopped and an excited radio announcer broke in with an urgent public message. "Attention! Our apologies to our listening audience for this interruption; however, a white supremacist who was recently convicted of the serial murder, rape, and cannibalism of young women has just escaped from the local maximum security prison. He is reported to have attacked one of the prison guards. The vicious criminal genius is described as a blond, Caucasian male with huge muscular arms. As a consequence, authorities are asking that any motorists stay off of Lakeshore Drive until he is captured. Now the marathon continues as we present a romantic musical interlude between Michael and Oprah!"

Bethany was listening to a soothing rendition of the duet from the film *Dirty Dancing*, when suddenly the dark sky flashed with distant lightning. Bethany was abruptly startled as she saw a large figure standing by her car. He was a blond, Caucasian man with huge muscular arms and he was wearing a soiled prison guard's uniform and he spoke with a thick Southern drawl. "Excuse me, ma'am. I did not mean to startle you." A clap of thunder rolled by as the strange man moved closer and added, "I thought perhaps I could offer you my help."

Bethany (or "Hey you forgot your purse again." as the checkout clerk at the health food store always called to her) smiled and said, "Why, how kind of you! Well if you happen to have a spare tire on you that would help a lot." Bethany laughed and added, "I am just kidding. Actually if it is not too much to ask, I would appreciate it if you could help me find my spare tire. I am just not very good with mechanical stuff."

The man scrutinized Bethany and he quickly sized her up as he replied, "I think that the cruel men who run the world hide the spare tire in the trunk to keep sweet, young women like yourself 'in their place,' so to speak. I'd be glad to change the tire for you, if you would be so kind as to give me a lift into town, Ma'am."

Bethany's faith in this kind, sensitive man grew. She glanced at his cracked nameplate and replied, "Why yes, I'd be happy to take you wherever you like. Allow me to introduce myself." Bethany stuck out her hand as she had learned at finishing school was the proper thing for a young lady to do around strangers. "My name is Bethany Louise and I am very pleased to meet you . . . Officer Jose Rodriguez."

Shaking Bethany Louise's hand with a forced smile, Jose said, "I'm pleased to meet you, too." Then, his frigid blue eyes flashed as he quickly explained, "You see, the nuns in the orphanage gave me this name. The other prison guards often kid me about it. At least they did not call me Sue. If you will be so kind as to open the trunk to your car, I'd be glad to get started, Miss Bethany Louise."

As Bethany walked by Jose, he quickly turned to follow. For a brief moment his shoulder lightly brushed against her full blouse as she caught her breath in pleasant surprise. She opened the trunk and seductively ran her fingers through her long soft curls. Jose pulled the spare tire out and quickly got to work. Inhaling deeply, Bethany could smell a strong manly scent with a slight hint of blood on Jose that almost caused her to swoon. Bethany Louise could hardly keep her eyes off of this intriguing stranger as he labored with the tools and jack. Suddenly, a cool autumn rain began to fall and Jose remarked, "Miss Bethany Louise, you'd better get in the car, now. You're starting to shiver." Jose wiped the grime from his hands onto his uniform pants and then he ran his strong hands up and down Bethany Louise's smooth arms as he added, "You are going to get wet all over."

Bethany wanted so badly to stay by Jose's side but reluctantly followed his advice. She entered her car and sat behind the steering wheel. Carefully, she adjusted the vehicle's side mirror to bring her rescuer into view. An uncontrollable desire overcame Bethany Louise to observe Jose as he toiled with her flat tire. He had taken off his shirt now, revealing his perfect frame. She could clearly see his tattooed arms now. Bethany bounced the tip of her index finger on her soft lips as she tried to remember from her college days which fraternity was known as "The Aryan Brotherhood." Louie Poo's thoughts raced through numerous romantic scenarios where Jose would be her knight in shining armor. She closed her eyes and imagined that their children would have her blond curls and his steely eyes. They would go to the beach and she and the kids would build castles in the sand. Then B Lo awoke from her day dreaming as the trunk was slammed shut. Jose opened the passenger door and climbed in next to her.

"I hope that you don't mind, but I found this towel in the trunk to dry off with, Bethany," Jose said.

Bethany could hardly take her eyes off of Jose as he rubbed the towel over his chiseled chest. "Why no, I don't mind one little bit, Jose. I used that old thing at my yoga class last night," Bethany replied. "But I'm forgetting my manners. I live just a short distance away from here. We could go to my place and you could dry off and warm up with some hot chocolate."

Bethany blushed that she had suggested something so provocative. Jose held the towel up to his nose and inhaled deeply like a predatory animal catching scent of its prey. He smiled and replied, "Bethany, I can hardly refuse such a generous invitation. I'd like that. I'd like that a lot." Then Jose began to slowly roll the towel up like a cord in his lap and tied an assassin's knot in the middle.

"Wake up and smell the coffee!" blared from the radio as Bethany switched the commercial off.

Bethany remarked, "Oh my, aren't you the creative one. You've folded that simple old towel of mine into what looks like some sort of garrote." Bethany Louise (or "Weezey" as Mr. Jefferson always called her in memory of his wife) remembered her days in Summer Theater as she explained, "If an evil villain were to wrap that around some sweet, innocent, young girl's throat and pulled on the ends as hard as he could, then the knot would crush her larynx." Bethany held one hand to her forehead in a melodramatic pose as she added with hoarse mock desperation, "The poor thing would not be able to cry out at all while she slowly suffocated to death."

Jose began to breathe excitedly as Bethany finished her performance, so she turned the defroster on. Then she remembered her Origami class and stated proudly, "I'll have you know that I'm very creative too. I can fold a chewing gum wrapper into a cute, little bunny rabbit." Her fingers danced playfully on the steering wheel as she whispered, "Hoppin' down the bunny trail . . ."

Then Bethany's face lit up as she remarked, "I could honor you as my house guest to a delicious, home-cooked meal that's totally my fave. Do you like liver with fava beans and a nice Chianti?"

Jose inhaled through his mouth and made a slow wooshing sound as his tongue quickly swished back and forth between his lips. Then he replied, "That's my fave too, Bethany."

"Woo hoo!" Bethany exclaimed as she clapped her hands together in childish excitement. Then she quickly regained her composure and placed both hands securely back on the steering wheel. She glanced over at Jose with her sweet, green eyes and remarked, "I don't mind telling you that I can sense something really special between us. I'm getting the feeling that this may be a night I will never forget."

Jose grinned and responded, "I'm beginning to feel the same way, Bethany. I know that this will be a night that I will never forget."

Bethany giggled with joy as she could no longer believe her good fortune. This was like the plot from some movie or romantic novel. The lightning flashed again and thunder roared ominously as she said, "You are such a dream come true for helping me out back there. My dear old dad would never believe this. He was always afraid that something horrible would happen to me."

Just then a black cat ran across in front of Bethany's car. She swerved around the feline at the last moment. The cat arched its back and screeched in shock as Bethany threaded her vehicle under a construction ladder that just happened to be by the side of the road. Bethany Louise nicked the ladder and the vehicle's side view mirror broke with a loud crunch. A large murder of dark crows flew over her car as she got it back on the road. Finally, she pulled up to a traffic light and signaled a left turn as she proceeded onto 13th Street.

Bethany Louise breathed easily as she exclaimed, "Wow! That sure was strange. I thought that all the birds had already gone south. That does remind me, though. I need to pick up something for Mr. Beasely."

Jose quickly considered Bethany's statement. He frowned and then asked, "Mr. Beasely? Is that your boyfriend, Bethany?"

Bethany blushed and replied, "Oh no. Mr. Beasely is my cat. He's a gray Egyptian Mau with a bent tail. I volunteer at a local animal shelter and he is a rescue. I like taking care of strays. I get bitten and scratched a lot at the shelter, but I just don't know when to quit. The other girls that volunteer even have funny nick names for me, like 'Bethany Loser' and 'Bethany Lousy with the wild pets' or 'Bet on Louise to let that big dog hump her leg again'. It's not so bad really. For instance, Mr. Beasely hasn't peed in my lap since yesterday. I am sure that you two will get along just fine." Then Bethany thought for a moment and added, "Just keep him off of your lap."

As Jose listened to Bethany's explanation he began to play with the tightly curled towel. Then his strong hand reached over and caressed Bethany's smooth arm once more as he said, "Miss Bethany, your flesh is so soft and tender . . . just the way I like it."

Bethany nodded her head in agreement as she remarked, "Yeah that is true. I really have not been doing my martial arts training like I used to."

Jose stopped abruptly and almost sheepishly asked, "You . . . you take martial arts training?"

Bethany shook her head back and forth and replied, "No, of course not." Jose was relieved to hear this and reached for the towel once again as Bethany added, "I only teach martial arts now, mostly to my little brother and his friends."

Jose dropped the towel as he considered this and asked gingerly, "So you mean to say that you teach martial arts to children?"

Bethany laughed and responded, "Sometimes it certainly does feel that way, but no, my bro' is a Ranger Instructor at the Jungle Warfare School for the United States Army. I believe his friends belong to the Green Berets and if I recall correctly, something called a sixth team of sea lions." Bethany shook her head again and added, "Whatever! I think that they are just a big bunch of candy butts if you ask me. They were all so cocky until I broke that Drill Sergeant's arm. I told Mr. Macho to tap out, but nooo. Oh my God, he was such a cry baby. Do you know that he wouldn't even let me sign his cast when I visited him in the hospital."

Bethany (or Mistress Pain as her obedient minions were now permitted to address her) pulled in to the parking lot by the health food store. She patted Jose on the shoulder and did her best Schwarzenegger impression as she said, "I'll be back." She quickly got all of the ingredients that she would need for her favorite meal. Then suddenly, as she stood in the check out line her hopes were dashed. She saw Jose running down the street in front of the health food store. She heard sirens as police cars descended on him from all sides. Armed police officers grabbed Jose and he was thrown into the back of a large padded van. The vehicles then sped away in the direction of the local penitentiary. Bethany concluded that Officer Rodriguez obviously must be some kind of important criminologist and was urgently needed for that thing at the prison.

She walked out to her car as the checkout clerk once again yelled to her about her purse. Bethany just shrugged her shoulders and said to herself, "I wonder if I will ever get laid."

LISA GOODMAN, WRITER

by Lynda Sappington

L isa admired the antique roll top desk she'd just spent an entire
day cleaning and polishing. "This desk is just what I need to
start my writing career," she said with satisfaction. With her legal
pads, index cards, an ink bottle and the handsome fountain pen she'd
found in one of the desk's hidden compartments lined up neatly on
the old-fashioned blotter, Lisa felt inspired. Many successful writers
before her had used such materials. One of the previous owners of the
desk, according to the auctioneer, had been a well-known mystery
writer. She'd probably used this very fountain pen. Lisa hoped it
would inspire her to write best-selling prose.

She gazed out of the window beside her desk at the depressing
view of long-neglected homes, abandoned warehouses and empty
office buildings that were the sad legacy of the recession in the
formerly prosperous city of Dayton, Ohio. Some of the ugliness was
masked by the long shadows and soft hues of the sunset's afterglow,
but still, what was once a bustling, prosperous town was spotted with
wastelands now, and her apartment overlooked some of them. She'd
grown up when National Cash Register, several GM and Chrysler
plants and their ancillary businesses were thriving. Unfortunately,
they all either closed or left the area as the economy soured.

Lisa had worked for the *Dayton Daily News* until it moved out of
the county and she couldn't afford the commute. The best job she
could find after that was as a clerk-typist at a hospital. Every day, she
had to drag herself to work at a job she hated. The only good thing
about the situation was that she made enough to pay her rent, even if
this shabby apartment in a dismal part of town was all she could
manage now.

She lucked into the desk in an estate sale where she was the only bidder on the filthy old thing. She still couldn't believe she'd gotten the roll top desk for such a good price, but she wasn't going to question it. She was determined to believe her luck had finally changed. Obtaining this now-beautiful desk was the first sign of that change, she was sure of it!

She turned up the radio when a particularly cheerful song started playing. Determined to start her story in the most positive frame of mind possible, she danced around her threadbare rug dreaming about holding her own published book in her hand, a line of people waiting for her to autograph the books they'd just purchased, and the red carpet grand opening of her novel's adaptation as a movie.

"I'm a *writer!* No more slaving away as a typist. I'll never have such a dead-end job again!" Never again would she have to worry about where the money would come from to pay her bills. "I'm gonna find a nice apartment," she sang, making her own lyrics for the song she was dancing to. "And health insurance, that's important. And a new *caaaaaar.*" She wailed this last, matching the singer on the radio, her arms stretched as wide as her dreams.

The phone rang. Lisa looked at it in disgust. Why did someone have to interrupt her lovely daydream? When she answered it, she heard the gruff voice of her landlord on the other end.

"You need to turn the radio down and stop stomping around up there," he told her.

Lisa did her best to stifle her growl. "Who complained this time?"

"Upstairs, downstairs, the people on each side of you. Keep it down."

She sighed. "All right."

Lisa turned the radio down and flopped on the couch as loudly as she could, hoping to disturb the neighbors just one more time. "I miss having a house. These walls are so thin, they can probably hear what I'm thinking."

"She thinks we can hear her think," her next door neighbor said with a loud, cackling laugh. This particular neighbor was old, nosy and well known for complaining to the manager about everything, especially noise in neighboring apartments.

"She's right, Clara. I reckon she can hear what we think too," her husband agreed.

"Yeah. What we're thinking is, 'Shut up!'" the woman said, then laughed with her husband.

Their voices came clearly through the wall, which didn't surprise Lisa. She'd moved to this building when the bank foreclosed on her mother's house. She'd even sold her mother's furniture to try to pay the bills, but the bills were sky-high, and her mom's furniture was just old, not good antique furniture, so it didn't bring much.

Lisa got up and walked over to her new desk, running her hand lovingly over the beautiful wood, then picked up the name plate she purchased when she first joined the staff of the *Dayton Daily News* right after graduating from college. She was so certain she'd be doing feature articles and interviews in no time, she thought the name plate would soon be in use, but she'd never gotten out of the advertising department. Lisa sighed with ever-present frustration. She was a good writer, but she'd never been given an opportunity to show what she could do. But now the name plate was perfect. She'd write some novels and do some freelance articles and make a name as a writer on her own. She didn't need the *Dayton Daily News* or any other newspaper to give her a start as a writer. She'd do it herself.

Holding tight to her visions of a brighter future, she put the nameplate on top of the desk. "Lisa Goodman, Writer." That's the way things were supposed to be. She felt a little flutter of happiness under her heart—or were those butterflies in her stomach as she wondered if she could still write beautiful prose after years of writing advertising drivel? She shook her head, defying her negative thoughts. She could still write, she was sure of it. She simply needed to get to work!

Lisa straightened her name plate a little before she sat down and uncapped the ink bottle to load the pen. When she held the fountain pen, she felt the same chill she felt whenever she was near the desk. The chill could be from the chilly evening outside, but she preferred to attribute it to her excitement at finally following her dream after so many years of mind-numbing, soul-killing work in the everyday world.

"Ouch!" There was a sharp edge she hadn't noticed on the clip on the fountain pen. She pushed away from the desk, leaving a smear of blood on the desk edge, then walked to her bathroom to put antiseptic and a bandage on the wound. Sighing at yet another delay in starting her writing career, she returned to her desk with a determined stride, a damp paper towel in her hand to clean up the blood that had dripped on its gleaming surface. She stared at the desk in disbelief. The blood was gone!

Lisa looked around. She was sure some blood had dripped onto the desk—or did it land on the floor? She pulled back her chair and bent down to look for bloodstains on the floor under the desk, but didn't find any there either.

Shrugging off her confusion, she tossed the towel in the trash, then sat down and finished filling the pen, being careful to avoid the sharp edge on the pen's fill lever. She would start a story tonight, she would! Nothing else was going to get in the way!

She pulled a legal pad toward her, excited about getting started on her novel, but then she shivered.

"Why is it always so cold in here? I can't afford to raise the thermostat. I guess I'll have to talk to the super again," she grumbled. "I'll do it tomorrow, though. Tonight is completely devoted to writing."

Grabbing a sweater from the closet, she shrugged it on, then moved back to the desk. She planned to write five hundred words before bedtime to get a good start on her story.

Lisa picked up the antique fountain pen, enjoying the weight of it in her hand. Somehow, it felt like quality. She smiled and started to write but suddenly felt a much stronger chill than before. Only four words in, she zipped up her sweater. Ten words in, she was shivering so hard, she went to her bedroom, dug some sweatpants out of a drawer, pulled them on over her jeans, then put on an extra pair of socks as well.

Finally, fifteen words filled a couple of lines, but her fingers and the paper were covered with drops of ink and her clothes were getting ink-splotched as well.

"So much for the romance of writing longhand," she muttered as she put the pen aside and went to wash up.

Clean again, Lisa plugged in her laptop and set it on the desk. She sighed as she stared at the blank screen, its cursor blinking patiently as it waited for her to begin.

The keyboard sat uncomfortably high on the desk, so Lisa raised her office chair and carried on. She tried to transcribe what she'd already written, but the words were so smeared, they were pretty much illegible. She gave up on them and started over, typing hesitantly at first, then smiling as her momentum increased. The old ways might seem romantic, but modern technology was much more efficient.

The story was finally starting to flow. Her computer screen was soon full of what she thought was pretty good prose—it was a decent start, anyway. When she hit "save," every word on the screen turned to gibberish.

"What the . . . ?" Her computer had never done that before. She closed the program, depending on its auto-save function to bring back the file she'd been working on. When she reopened it, there it was.

"That's a relief." She hit "save" again, resulting in a screen full of garbled words. She clicked "undo" and the correct words reappeared.

"I've never heard of a computer acting up this way." She hit "print" and two pages of garbage printed out. "No, no, no, no, NO!" She shoved her chair back from the desk and stormed around the room until she could approach her computer without wanting to throw it out of the window.

"What's wrong with you?" she demanded when she sat down in front of it again. The computer sat there complacently, its cursor blinking innocently as always.

She looked at the word count at the bottom of the screen and signed. *I'm only halfway to my five hundred word goal. I need to keep going.* She sighed again, mentally grumbling about how much harder writing was as a profession than people thought it was.

Getting a flash drive out of a drawer, Lisa inserted it in the computer, hoping a miracle would occur and the file would save properly to the flash drive even if it was garbled on screen. She was no good at fixing computers. She'd have to ask a friend who was pretty much a computer wizard for help, but he was camping in the mountains of Tennessee where he had no Internet or mobile phone connection. He went there every year, saying it was good for him to spend a week "unplugged." She hated the thought of having to wait to talk to him about her computer problems, but she couldn't afford to take the computer to a store for repair. Her friend would fix it in exchange for a home-cooked meal, a price Lisa could afford.

As she got back into the story, words crawled across her screen at a steady clip with only brief hesitations every so often as she searched for a better way to say something. The act of writing was helping her to organize her story in her mind, so she kept going despite the computer foul-ups.

An ache in her back finally made her stop typing. She pushed back from her desk, wondering if she'd be able to save her work this time. She hit "save" and got the same mess as before.

"Save, damn it!" She clicked "undo," then "save" again after the words appeared properly. "Again with the garbage?" She clicked "undo" and the words appeared again. She saved her work to the flash drive and went to bed without checking to see how it saved. She was thoroughly disgusted with her laptop and how much extra work modern technology brought to her life.

***

After a long, hard day of typing difficult medical terminology into charts at the hospital, Lisa was looking forward to typing what she wanted. As soon as possible after getting home, she sat at her desk and worked on her story. It still wouldn't save properly either on the hard drive or the flash drive, but she finally got a draft of it to print. Lisa scanned the printout into the computer, then opened that file so she could start work where she'd left off. When she started typing, it all turned to gibberish again. She rebooted her computer and discovered the scanned files were corrupted.

Sighing heavily, Lisa decided to start over. She rebooted the computer again, wrote a few lines of nonsense and tried to save it. Success!

"Why didn't it work when I rebooted it before? How bizarre." She shrugged and began working on her story again in a much more cheerful frame of mind. Having a cooperative computer was a great mood-lifter. At least what she'd done the night before had helped her get her thoughts more organized. Hopefully the work would flow more easily now.

The strong chill she'd felt the previous evening ran up her back again and her fingers started flying across the keys. The colder she was, the more blank her brain felt, and the faster she typed. Her hands were moving so quickly, she never even considered getting up to put a sweater on.

Words scrolled across the screen, elegant prose, but completely foreign to anything Lisa had ever written or even thought before, which was a shock to her. She shook her head, trying to release herself from whatever seemed to be controlling her. The cold just intensified, her fingers typing faster and faster.

***

Hours later, Lisa fell back in exhaustion, her chair nearly toppling over as her body's balance changed. She pushed back from the roll top desk, stood up and stretched, trying to get the kinks out of her back and neck.

"What was *that*?" She stared at the indicator bar at the bottom of the software's window. It showed nearly 20,000 words. How was that possible?

Lisa scratched her head, completely baffled. She sat back down, hit the "go to" command, went to page one and started reading. The story was good, really good, and absolutely terrifying. It was a murder mystery, something she'd never considered writing. The words used, the sentence structure, everything about it was completely unlike any of Lisa's previous writing. After reading two chapters, she sat back in awe.

"This desk really is inspiring!" she said, clapping her hands together gleefully. Red droplets splattered her glasses, startling her. She stared in shock at her hands. They were streaked with blood. *What the . . . how did I get hurt?* Pushing back from the desk, she stumbled to the bathroom to wash.

As pink-tinged soapy water swirled down the drain, she gasped when she realized there wasn't a scratch on her hands anywhere. She whirled around and stared at the desk sitting innocently in her office, its polished wood gleaming in the light from her laptop screen and the lamp on the desk's shelf. She'd worked so long, most of the lighted windows she could normally see in nearby apartment buildings were dark. She blinked and shook her head as she noticed the blood spattered on the desk's surface wasn't drying, but instead seemed to be being absorbed into the wood. She rubbed her eyes and looked again. Now there was no blood left on the desk at all, although many of the laptop's keys and the touchpad were smeared with blood.

Feeling more than a little frantic, she tried to calm herself. "I must have imagined that. Right?" The only reply she got, of course, was silence. There was no one there to answer her. A nervous laugh escaped her. "I really need to get a cat so I have someone to talk to."

Still chuckling uneasily at the ramblings of her mind, Lisa looked at her watch. Midnight. She'd worked through dinnertime, but she wasn't really hungry. She couldn't wait to get back to work on her story. But the blood on her hands was worrisome. How did it get there? As she re-entered her office area, she noticed muddy footprints from her desk to the bathroom on the ratty old fake Persian rug no one would bid on at her mother's estate auction. Torn between anger and fear, she spun around and saw the same muddy footprints in a trail from the bathroom to where she was standing. Looking down, she noticed her shoes were not only muddy but wet. She'd been out in the rain that continued to pound on her windowpanes. Why? Where had she gone? And when? She couldn't remember moving from her desk since she'd started typing just after she got home from work.

Looking around some more, she saw muddy footprints going to her desk from the front door of her apartment. She went to the door and opened it, to find the knob smeared with bits of blood on the back of the knob where the neighbors wouldn't be as likely to notice. She must have wiped off the front of the knob when she came in. The footprints led from the outside door of her building, up the two flights of stairs to her apartment and right to her door.

Shaken by her findings, Lisa went back inside her apartment to think. She couldn't remember going outside. She didn't remember putting on her raincoat, which hung dripping from a hook behind the front door. She had no idea when or why she'd gone out.

Doing her best to calm her nerves, Lisa grabbed her broom and dustpan, then went out to sweep up the drying mud from the hall carpet and stairs so the trail wouldn't lead directly to her door anymore. When her sweeping took her near the front door, a couple stumbled in, obviously drunk. They looked at her blearily.

"Why're you sweepin' here?" the woman said, her words slurred, her face furrowed with suspicion.

"I was chasing a mouse out of my apartment," Lisa said. When the woman squealed and clung more closely to her companion, Lisa added, "It ran out when you opened the door."

"It's gone?" the man said, rubbing a shaky hand over his face, then peering at her blearily.

Lisa smiled as sincerely as she could manage. "Yes. Thanks for opening the door just then. It was a big help."

The man waved dismissively. "Happy t'help. G'night."

"Night," Lisa replied, watching them drag themselves up the stairs. After they disappeared behind the fire door to the second floor, Lisa blew out a nervous breath, then went back to work on the carpet to get every trace of dried mud out of the carpet nap. She smeared around the mud that was too damp to sweep so it was no longer recognizable as footprints.

She realized the couple had also tracked in some mud from the filthy sidewalk in front of their building, deposited there by the construction work on the road near their building. She sighed in relief then removed her still-dirty shoes and returned to her flat.

"One-thirty in the morning. No wonder I'm tired." She set her broom back in the corner where it belonged, then took her shoes and a small scrub brush to the kitchen trash can, opened the lid, then went to work on their caked-on mud. When they were finally clean enough to suit her, she set them down and dragged her exhausted body to bed, falling on top of the duvet still fully clothed.

***

And so the days passed, with Lisa going to work in the morning as usual, spending the day typing up medical records. After work, she'd rush home start working on her story as soon as she could get to her desk, typing long into the night, losing track of time just as she had the first evening. Whenever she once more became aware of her surroundings, she was bone-weary and terribly chilled. She never found her hands or shoes horribly bloody again, but once in a while she'd find a spot of blood on her shoes, although there were still no wounds anywhere on her body, not even a scratch.

Her story was becoming an epic-length novel. The writing and plot were terrifying and fascinating at the same time. Lisa never considered writing a murder mystery before, but it was just flying out of her fingers into her laptop, often much faster than she'd ever typed before.

This pattern went on for a few weeks before Lisa overheard a newscast in the break room at the hospital where she worked. A mutilated body was found behind a hotel in Miamisburg. She felt a chill as the details emerged. When the story finished, she hurried back to her desk, dug her backup flash drive out of her purse and jammed it into her computer to look at her novel. The sketchy details given during the newscast were eerily close to the details of one of the murders in her story.

Dumbfounded, she stared at the screen in shock until the sound of a door slamming down the hall snapped her out of her stupor. She shook her head hard, trying to clear it, then shrugged. "Just a strange coincidence," she murmured, determinedly ignoring the chill racing up and down her spine.

That evening, Lisa stayed away from her desk. Instead, she sat on her couch, remote in hand, and flipped channels on the TV until she found something to watch that wasn't too challenging for her weary brain. She drifted somewhere between sleep and wakefulness as her mind picked at the similarities between the news story and her novel. Eventually she fell into a fitful sleep on the couch with the TV still on.

Hours later, Lisa was awakened by the morning sun streaming through her window. She stared at the laptop in front of her. When did she move to the desk? Her hands were freezing. She rubbed them together anxiously as she wondered what happened. She pushed back from the desk to get something to eat and noticed blood on her shoes, a lot of it this time. She sat there and stared at her shoes in shocked silence for several long moments.

"In breaking news," the anchorman on the morning news show said, "another body has been found. Let's go to Susan Quinn, who is on site where the body was discovered. Susan?"

A pretty young woman with long blond hair, beautiful eyes and perfect teeth smiled into the camera, then switched to a more serious expression. "Thanks, Dan. We're here in Possum Creek Park with Sergeant Mike Fellows of the Dayton Police Department. Sergeant Fellows, what can you tell us about the crime?"

The stern-faced police officer standing beside the reporter said, "The victim appears to have been in her thirties. The coroner says she died last evening. We think she was jogging in Possum Creek Park when she was killed. She carried no identification but she's a white woman with red hair and brown eyes. She was wearing a blue and white jogging suit."

"Thank you, Sergeant Fellows," the perky reporter said, turning away from him. "The coroner has established that the body that was found yesterday died between three and four weeks ago. The police believe these two deaths could be related. If you know anything about these incidents or the identity of the most recent victim, please contact the police."

Lisa shut off the TV. Possum Creek Park. Years ago, Lisa used to take her niece to a pond in that park so she could feed the ducks. That was before her sister and brother-in-law, like everyone else in Lisa's family with a grain of sense and some money saved, moved somewhere where there were more and better jobs available.

She shivered, thinking Dayton was becoming too dangerous to enjoy anymore. Then again, when was the last time she was at the park? It wasn't long ago. She remembered feeding the ducks at dusk recently, but couldn't remember when.

She went to the closet and grabbed the jacket she wore the most this time of year. In one pocket was the wrapper from a bag of popcorn she'd taken to feed the ducks. She remembered sitting on the bench and enjoying the evening, then feeding the ducks when they swam near her. She was sure she'd stayed until it was fully dark, which wasn't normal for her. Why did she do that? She shook her head, trying hard to remember. At dusk, there was a runner, a woman with a long red ponytail. The way the setting sun made the woman's ponytail look like liquid fire fascinated Lisa as she watched the woman jog by.

Lisa pulled off her shoes and padded over to kitchen sink where she scrubbed at the bloody spots on her shoes until her hands were raw and sore. After dabbing at the shoes with paper towels to try to dry them and then drying her hands, she moved to her desk and opened the chapter she'd written last night.

"Sharon sat in the park by the pond, enjoying the feeding frenzy as the ducks scrambled to get the popcorn she was tossing in the water before the fish could.

A woman jogged by, her long red ponytail glimmering like fire in the light of the low-riding sun. She admired the woman's athletic build and how nicely her powder blue and white jogging suit fit her. Sharon had never been built like that. Never. Her frizzy brown hair had never gleamed in the sunlight like that, had never flowed like silk on the wind that way. Sharon found herself resenting the woman's beauty and easy grace. She sighed, then dug in her large tote bag for more popcorn as the jogger disappeared around a bend in the trail.

"Some time later, the redhead came jogging down the path again, as Sharon knew she did every day. This time, Sharon was hiding behind a tree. As the jogger passed, Sharon grabbed that flowing, fiery ponytail and jerked, pulling the woman off-balance. With the woman's throat opened to the sky, Sharon slashed that inviting target from one side to the other, then proceeded to stab her repeatedly. The jogger's pretty face was sliced to ribbons, her body riddled with wounds.

Sharon reveled in the feeling of power that surged through her. This pretty, well-dressed, beautifully groomed woman wasn't a match for Sharon. Sharon was strong, she was powerful, she vanquished foes with one slash of her knife!

"Take that, bitch," she muttered as she wiped the blood off her knife onto the woman's pretty blue and white jogging suit.

When Sharon finished, she stood up and removed the medical

scrubs she'd pulled over her clothes, wiping her face and hands with them before stuffing them in a plastic bag. As she left her killing ground, Sharon drove to the hospital where she worked and went to the surgical wing. Once there, she dumped the scrubs in the proper bins where they'd mingle with dozens of others just like them."

***

Lisa's hands trembled as they hovered over the keyboard. Did *she* do it? How could she have done it? She didn't remember any violence, no details of the murder except for seeing the jogger by the pond. Lisa was a gentle soul. She'd never even considered hurting anyone before. What happened?

She shook her head, a shaky laugh escaping as she realized how ridiculous it was to think she was a killer. Lisa couldn't explain what was going on, but she decided a state of denial was probably her best choice for now. She shoved every thought about murders, blood, her story and anything else scary in her head into the farthest corner of her mind, to be considered later when she was calmer.

Lisa took a slow, deep breath trying to calm herself, then wiped the tears from her face and held a cold, wet cloth to her aching eyes, hoping she'd stop crying soon. She tried to calm herself, then remembered she was safe with all the bad thoughts shoved safely into that corner. She'd be fine. Yes, she would.

Closing the roll top desk, Lisa locked it with her powered-off, unplugged laptop inside. She put the desk's key in the back of the linen closet where it would be hard to reach. Now she couldn't get to the laptop, she couldn't write and hopefully she wouldn't go wandering off during the night to kill people. She shook her head at the thought of *her* being a killer. Ridiculous! She simply wasn't getting enough sleep. That was it. The exhausted mind could come up with all kinds of crazy ideas.

Lisa took a sleeping pill and went to bed, hoping to get a decent amount of sleep for a change. Writing was fun but it wasn't worth this kind of worry, and certainly not worth the lives of those who had been killed. No, she couldn't think of those poor souls, or she'd never sleep again. She shoved them into that corner of her mind too, a shaky laugh escaping as she pondered the wild thoughts she'd been having. She couldn't possibly be a killer. No way. She got upset if she needed to kill a fly or a spider in her apartment. How could she possibly kill a human being? She couldn't, and that was the truth. She was too involved in her story, that was it. Time away from it would be good for her.

The things she was trying to hide from herself glowed in the back corner of her mind, teasing her, tempting her to dig them out again.

Lisa brushed her teeth with serious intensity, cleansed her face, slathered it with moisturizer, combed out her hair and went to bed, turned out the light and settled in for a good night's sleep, stubbornly ignoring the bright light in what was supposed to be the darkest corner of her mind.

***

Early the next morning, Lisa awoke to find herself at her desk, her nails torn, her hands bruised and scratched, with blood on the lid of the roll top desk. Apparently she'd tried to open it with her bare hands.

"Foiled your plans, didn't I?" Lisa said with a shaky laugh, glaring at the desk. "It's you, isn't it? I heard people at the auction saying you were haunted, but I didn't believe them. But they're right, aren't they? Is there a writer's ghost in there who wrote mysteries based on real killings?"

There was no answer. Of course there wasn't. She was talking to a desk! A strangled laugh came out of her before she started beating her fists on the desk's slatted cover. "What have you done?" She dropped her forehead on her fists and sobbed. "What have *I* done?"

She sat up, shoved her chair back from the desk and stared at it in horror when she heard the muted sound of her laptop's keys clicking along merrily.

Lisa stood on shaking legs and went to the linen closet and dug out the key. When she neared the desk again, she heard the keys still tapping away. Blowing out a nervous breath, she shoved the key in the lock and opened the desk. There sat her laptop, typing all by itself, her novel on the screen having line after line of well-written yet horrifying prose added to it as she watched.

"Why are you doing this to me?" Lisa screamed. She stared in shock as a new paragraph scrolled across the monitor.

"You said you wanted to be a writer. We're helping you write a publishable novel. There was no chance in hell that the drivel you were writing at the start would ever catch a publisher's eye."

"I didn't ask for your help!" Lisa cried.

"You asked for help the first night when you dripped blood onto the desk after using the pen. Now we are bound together."

Lisa stepped farther from the desk, wringing her hands anxiously. "Who are you?"

"This desk has been owned by many writers, each more famous than the ones before. At various times, we shed our blood on the desk as we pursued our dream, and we became linked with it. Powerful prose comes from deep wells of emotion, from passion, grief, pain. You are filled with those things. We've drawn on those parts of you and shared our own with you as our gift for restoring the desk."

Lisa backed up until the wall stopped her. "No! I don't want your help. Leave me alone!"

"You lived a colorless life and had no inspiration. We gave that to you."

"By killing people? How could you?"

"The deeds are done, the novel is nearly finished, and the rest shall soon be history."

"No! I won't allow it!" Lisa cried.

"You won't allow it?" appeared on the screen. "Then our help to you is at an end. On your head be it."

"You're just a figment of my imagination," Lisa cried as she stared at the monitor in horror. "You don't have any power over me or anything else. I can will you away like that." She snapped her fingers.

"We can make you successful, or we can ruin you. It's your choice," scrolled across the screen.

"I don't need or want your help."

"So be it." With that, the typing stopped.

Lisa growled in frustration. "Stupid imagination playing tricks on me. Stupid computer talking back to me." She paced across the floor, frantic thoughts chasing each other through her mind. "I'm not getting enough rest, that has to be it. How do I fix this?" She looked around her apartment for a moment before running into the building's hallway. Near the fire alarm, she found the glass-covered box that held a fire hose and an ax. She broke the glass protecting the ax, then carried the heavy implement back to her apartment and began chopping the desk and laptop both into pieces. She ignored the metallic shrieks and crackly noises coming from the laptop and the groaning of the desk as she dismembered them, just as she was ignoring the awful aches in her muscles from swinging the ax over and over.

Grabbing some large garbage bags, she cleaned up the mess, then carried the bags to her car parked behind the building. She drove out into the rural area west of Dayton until she found a patch of woods near a country road she'd taken at random. She dragged the bags into the center of the small forest and removed the broken pieces, throwing them as far as she could in every direction. With the amount of rain they'd had lately, hopefully the chunks of wood and plastic would soon sink into the mud so they'd be buried forever.

As each piece of the now-hated desk and laptop sailed out of sight, she breathed a little easier. Whatever made her write that novel was out of her life now. She wouldn't even consider what else that possessing power might have forced her to do. She wouldn't think about it. She shoved those thoughts and fears into that dark corner of her mind.

As she walked back to her car, she wondered if she should call the police. Her stomach clenched violently when she realized there was no proof of her innocence now that she'd destroyed the laptop and desk. She'd never convince anyone the laptop talked back to her, that some spirit from the desk had written the novel and done all those horrible things. The police would blame her for those murders and it wasn't her fault! A wave of nausea overwhelmed her and she vomited. She wiped her mouth with a tissue and forced all the bad thoughts into the darkest corner of her mind. Once they were put away, she began to calm down. It wasn't her fault. It was clearly the fault of that demented desk.

***

The woman whose apartment was next to the fire equipment on Lisa's floor banged on the door to the building manager's apartment. "Mr. Lambert? Mr. Lambert! Open up! This time that woman's gone too far."

"Good morning," Lambert said, trying to be pleasant to the belligerent woman. "What can I do for you?"

"You can evict that Lisa Goodman, that's what you can do! At the crack of dawn today, she broke the glass over the fire ax and started chopping something up in her apartment, screaming all the while! The noise was awful. And she left glass all over the floor."

Mr. Lambert frowned in concern. "Was there a fire?"

"No. She was chopping something up. I'll bet she murdered somebody and was disposing of the body! People do that. I've seen it on TV."

"I'll check it out," he said, following her back to her floor. He knocked on Lisa's door, but she wasn't home. While he was knocking, the neighbor woman was still complaining loudly. Other doors opened down the hallway, the occupants peeking out to see what was going on. Soon they all congregated around Mr. Lambert, who was still knocking on Lisa's door.

"Mr. Lambert, are you going to make her stop acting crazy?"

Lisa's next-door neighbor demanded.

"What do you mean? She's a nice tenant."

Several other neighbors began to speak at once. "She's a lunatic!"

"Runs up and down the stairs at all hours, wears strange clothes out and comes back in different clothes."

"She talks to herself, laughs and sings, and all of it loudly, but she complains if she hears us talking normally."

"We saw her sweeping the lobby in the middle of the night one time," a woman from the second floor said. "She said she'd chased a mouse out of her apartment, but I don't believe it."

The stories went on and on, growing more bizarre with each telling. The manager finally decided to call the police.

A short time later, the police came and took statements from everyone who offered them. They left an officer to watch Lisa's apartment. A few hours later, he contacted his superiors to let them know Lisa was home.

"What do you want?" Lisa said as she opened the door, stunned to see so many police officers facing her with aggression in their eyes.

Lisa's stomach clenched, but she put on as brave a face as she could manage. "Yes?"

"We'd like to ask you a few questions, ma'am. May we come in?"

Her heart was pounding wildly now. "Questions? About what?" What did they know? How could they know anything, and so fast?

"Someone reported seeing someone matching your description in the vicinity of the crime scene where the jogger was killed," the officer replied. "We have several statements that have given us probable cause to search your apartment. This is a search warrant." He handed her a piece of paper.

As soon as Lisa stepped back, her apartment was full of men in blue uniforms who seemed to take up entirely too much space.

"What do you want?"

The officer who'd spoken to her took out a small notebook and a pen while the other police officers started digging through her possessions.

"Where were you last night about eight PM?"

"I . . . I was here."

"Can anyone corroborate that?"

"I live alone."

"I've got something," a young policeman said.

"Let me see," the first officer said.

Lisa felt her blood pounding in her temples. She'd cleaned out the printer tray and shredded that story, she was sure of it. But there stood that young officer with several hundred printed pages in his hands. Lisa hadn't noticed the printout in the printer tray that morning. She wondered for a moment if her conversation with the desk was included.

After reading just a few pages, finding a box of scrubs in Lisa's closet and seeing a pair of stained shoes still drying on her kitchen counter, they arrested her. When they handcuffed her, Lisa's brain shut down. She couldn't answer any of their questions. She just kept rambling on about a roll top desk that ruined her life.

***

Hopeful writer Lisa Goodwin sat hugging herself in a small room with cushioned walls. Stories raced through her mind, making her long for her laptop. But her hands were tied. There was no way she could have one. Nor was she allowed a legal pad, note cards or anything else to help her write her stories. So she sat there alone, babbling her stories aloud. Every single one began as a sweet romance or a tale of lost love, but soon became a story filled with one horrific slaying after another. She shrugged, as much as she could in a straight jacket, and started another story. Eventually, she'd get one of them right. She was sure of it.

***

In a patch of woods on a farm in western Montgomery County, Ohio, a young woman exclaimed in excitement when she saw a beautiful roll top desk sitting in pristine condition in the center of the woods.

"What are you doing here? You're gorgeous! I'm taking you home!" A moment later, she frowned uncertainly as the desk seemed to move slightly, the slats of its roll top taking on the appearance of a slight, but very smug, smile.

NOSE ART

by Philip A. Lee

Benson's head was pounding when he came to in the restroom stall, painfully leaning at a very uncomfortable slant against the angular piping on the back of the toilet. He'd picked the wrong day to forget to take his meds, and all it took was the right low-blood-sugar attack to hit. One moment he was fully cognizant and awake, and then he must've lost consciousness. His body had surrendered to gravity, and he'd smashed his forehead against the stall door so hard in the small space that he'd rebounded and fallen back to settle against the chrome flush knob now digging into his lower back.

Everything took on a glassy quality as he soldiered through the pain long enough to sit up straight. The agony only evoked memories of him getting spritzed with shrapnel from a poorly maintained fuel tank that had ruptured at an airstrip over in Iraq. He was back home on medical discharge now, though—no more explosions or airplane mishaps to worry about, thankfully. Forcing his consciousness beyond the hazy barrier of oblivion, he made himself decent and staggered out the stall door to study himself in the mirror.

One massive knot graced his forehead. He found it hard to the touch, and just grazing it with his fingertip nearly made him pass out again. He sighed. There'd be no easy way to explain this one to his friends, and he'd never live it down even if he tried.

Walking out of the bathroom, he was startled at how dark he found the hallway. And still. Deathly still. The overhead lights were dimmed in most places, completely turned off in others. Shadow and silence replaced recent memories of kids running through the hall and swooshing around plastic airplanes or space shuttles from the gift shop. As far as he could tell, he had only been in the bathroom a few minutes to catch a quick moment of relief before heading back home, before closing time. The darkness meant not only had the museum closed, but the sun had also set, which meant he'd been out cold for at least an hour. When he checked his cell phone to see just how late it was, the screen came back black and lifeless.

This is how Benson Caulfield found himself locked in the National Museum of the United States Air Force after hours, alone.

Panic set in. Museum staff had likely missed him in their pre-closing sweep of this particular bathroom, considering he'd chosen the stall at the very back, the bottom of which couldn't easily be seen by a cursory glance from the door. And if there were any guards still making rounds—as if someone could *seriously* steal the SR-71 Blackbird after hours, he thought with an eye roll—they would arrest him for trespassing. Or worse, they might drag him straight to federal court.

Benson passed through the dimly lit gift shop, turned where he recalled the bronze statue of Icarus used to be displayed a few years back, and confronted the series of glass doors leading to the parking lot—empty, save for his lonely car parked way in the back.

He nonchalantly tried to exit and nearly sprained his shoulder as the door stood fast. The keyhole on the door was one of those special locks requiring a particular key, not a pin-and-tumbler style that could be picked with a bobby pin and some luck. And he couldn't smash through the glass. That would attract police and jail time, and it'd be impossible to prove he was breaking *out*, not breaking *in*.

Phones in the gift shop seemed to be wired for internal use only, and dialing 9-1-1 resulted in an automated message saying that extension did not exist. The only plan of action he devised that didn't end with him being arrested meant finding some innocuous place to hunker down for the night, waiting until the museum reopened, blending in with the first group of visitors, and then making a graceful exit.

But he couldn't sleep. If his forehead egg was indeed a

concussion, falling asleep for any extended period of time might kill him.

Although guilt ate at him for doing so, he raided the gift shop for a few pouches of astronaut ice cream, a bottle of caffeinated pop, and a coffee-table book of his favorite airplanes. Consciousness ammunition—he'd pay for them in the morning. Under one of the cash registers, he found a flashlight, which was a godsend considering his usually bright cell phone display was dead, and to hide the suspicious knot on his forehead from morning visitors, he grabbed a ball cap embroidered with an image of a P-38J Lightning.

The whole time, he came across not a single sign of security—no distant flashlights, no actively scanning cameras with flashing red eyes. As best he could tell, he had the whole museum to himself, and that was fine by him. His parents and siblings found the museum boring, so he often came here alone, if only for a gentle reminder of the military career his injuries had cut short and as his way of remembering those whose lives were still on the line every day.

The only thing he disliked about the museum was all the random mannequins scattered about, each one trapped in some manufactured moment such as fixing a plane or herding prisoners onto a cattle car. Something about them fell too far into the uncanny valley and sent chills down his spine. In the few floodlights that the staff had left on in the main hangars housing the collection, these disturbing faces took on an even eerier quality.

With so much time on his hands before the museum reopened, Benson decided to read every word of every placard and sign in his favorite gallery. He always found the hangar showcasing the Wright brothers and World War I aircraft fascinating, but his true historical love lay in the Allied struggle against the Axis powers in World War II. A large part of that love he attributed to a quirky paradigm change in how United States Army Air Force crews expressed their individuality.

Over the years Benson had collected photographs of World War II

-era nose art from various museums across the country, but the selection here always ranked among his favorite due to its proximity to his hometown. He passed quite a few familiar pieces: a winged boxcar, a skull-and-crossbones with the plane's actual machine guns poking through its eye sockets, the reclining blonde pinup girl on the side of the Boeing B-17G *Shoo Shoo Baby*, a pink cartoon elephant holding a four-leaf clover next to the words "Five by Five," the imposing shark face and eyes on the Curtiss P-40E Warhawk . . . Eventually he meandered down the path until he stopped at one of his favorite planes in the museum's collection, a rusty-pink bomber with an impressive wingspan and one of the largest and most eye-catching pieces of nose art he had ever seen.

She was a beaut, and he wasn't talking about the two-dimensional redhead in the blue ruffle dress lounging on the plane's starboard fuselage, although she was an added bonus. A Consolidated B-24D Liberator—"AIR FORCES SERIAL NO. 42-72843," according to the black stenciled paint on its side—affectionately known by her crew as the *Strawberry Bitch*.

Forget interceptors or attack fighters. Before his military proficiency assessment consigned him to airfield ground staff, Benson had always envisioned himself part of a bomber's crew complement because teamwork felt more rewarding than personal glory. He had no problem leaving fighter piloting to the showboaters.

As he drew closer to the Liberator's fuselage, he admired the playful, Vargas-esque pinup girl, a reminder to the illusion of a different, more innocent time. Even in the dim light he could make out the brush strokes of the artist who had lovingly restored the image. But then something about the texture changed. Whether it was his pounding head or a trick of the light, he couldn't be sure, but there was no mistake.

The paint was moving.

Heart racing, he stumbled backwards while watching the image inexplicably bubble outward like simmering liquid in a saucepan. Just as he ducked behind a nearby plane, he poked his head out long enough to witness the pinup girl peel right off the side of the Liberator like a vinyl window cling and flutter towards the ground— and walk upright on a pair of black, peep-toe high heels.

Flat.

Two-dimensional.

Benson blinked. At that moment, he knew he'd stumbled right into a dream. This was either some nightmare gone wrong or he'd smashed his head harder than he thought. A light yet agonizing touch to his throbbing forehead reminded him this was indeed real. When he turned away and looked back, the flattened girl was still standing there, now yawning and stretching toward the hangar's ceiling as though she'd just woken from a far-too-long nap. Her every movement felt akin to single frames of hand-drawn animation rather than manifesting as folded or crinkling paper when her arms and legs moved—a living painting capable of redrawing itself at will.

From around the large, olive-drab B-17, a modestly topless, leggy blonde in a floral beach wrap sashayed over to chat with the redhead like they were old friends. Her body, Benson saw, also proved as thin as a single layer of aircraft paint, even in profile. A third girl, a strawberry blonde, seemed lost in thought as her powder blue blouse seemed frozen in a perpetual state of near-removal. A brunette in a blue swimsuit and strappy heels soon wandered in with a corded phone pressed up to her ear. She would talk into the receiver then share something with the other girls before laughing and resuming her phone conversation. Only problem was, the phone cord ended after about three feet. That, and the girl looked like a steamroller had run over her.

Once the knee-high pink elephant rollicked into view proudly displaying its little four-leaf clover clutched in its trunk, Benson was convinced he'd utterly lost his mind. He couldn't help but chuckle from the absurdity. All of these images he'd seen countless times on various planes throughout the museum. Floral Skirt was from the

Shoo Shoo Baby, just around the bend. Strawberry Blonde hailed from a Douglas A-26C Invader in the opposite corner. Chatty Cathy, from a Republic F-105D Thunderchief called the *Memphis Belle II*, over in the Southeast Asia War gallery.

And the elephant? Straight from the Republic P-47D Thunderbolt just a few planes down the path. Benson nearly laughed out loud at the thought.

The redhead perked up in his direction. "Someone there?" she said in a voice surprisingly unlike what he'd expected from some phantom who'd just walked off the side of a vintage airplane. Instead, she sounded like an actress from some movie in the '40s or '50s. Sweet. Classy. And just a touch of Southern flair. Completely non-threatening.

Benson scratched his temple and walked out into the open. "Uh, hi," he said.

"Well hello, darlin'," she said. "Ain't never seen you 'round here before. Where you from?"

"Dayton," he said, "born and raised." He instantly felt like a fool. Talking with a—a what? A figment of his imagination? A fever dream? A ghost?

"No, I mean which plane are you from? Some new acquisition? Or are you from the Annex?"

He shook his head. "I'm . . . I'm not from a plane."

The B-17 girl gasped and touched the redhead on the shoulder. "He's a *visitor*, Red!" she said in an incredulous whisper. "I don't trust him."

"Easy, Shoo," the redhead said with an infectious chuckle. "No need to be jumpin' to conclusions. Maybe . . . maybe he can help us."

"Why would he? He's not one of us."

Ignoring the blonde, Red said, "So, what's your name, handsome?"

I am talking to a piece of nose art, Benson had to remind himself. The very idea was ludicrous, yet, there she was, standing in front of him in all of her two-dimensional glory, her painted lips moving, her eyes absorbing everything going on around her.

"Benson," he said at length. "Benson Caulfield, Senior Airman, United States Air Force. Uh, *former* Senior Airman, that is."

She smiled. "Pleased to meetcha, Benny. You can call me Red. This here is Shoo. The bird over on the telephone, her name's Gabby. And the gal havin' problems with her top is Dream. Fivers, Patches, and all the other Mascots call us the Femmes."

Benson rubbed his headachy eyes one more time. If this was indeed an elaborate fantasy, all of these characters should disappear when he opened his eyes. But Red and the other apparitions were still there, still gauging his reaction. This was real, right down to the flying pink elephant that was no larger than a medium-sized dog.

He laughed out loud to spite his slow descent into inevitable madness. Brain damage, he thought. Exposure to some undisclosed nerve agent he might have encountered out in the Middle East. His laughter echoed and carried through the high rafters of the hangar.

Red's mortified face went paler than it already was. "Keep it down," she chided in a near whisper. "You don't wanna wake up ol' Bocksie, now do ya?"

Bocksie? Did she mean the *Bockscar*? The bomber that dropped the Fat Man on Nagasaki? Benson caught sight of the pink elephant— Fivers, Red had called him—which seemed far too happy for its own good cavorting about the place, and chuckled at his own logical conclusion. The nose art on the *Bockscar* depicted a railroad freight car aloft on small white wings, flying above a tiny representation of Nagasaki's mushroom cloud. Harmless as a pink elephant.

But then he recalled the other nose art on other planes in this gallery and in the other hangars.

Azrael, "Angel of Death"—a ghostly, Gatling-gun-toting skeleton gracing the side of the carrier-turned-gunship AC-130 Spectre.

Night Mare, the silhouette of a bucking bronco straight from the depths of Hell.

The gaping P-40 shark mouth.

The A-20 Havoc's grinning skull with machine guns pointing out of its eyeholes.

He shook his head to banish the thought. "Unless I misheard, you gals said you need help with something?"

"Shoo?" Red said. "You wanna spill the beans?"

As the blonde wandered closer to Benson, he marveled at how, no matter at what angle she was standing, something—a judiciously placed arm, hand, or the edge of a plane or another Femme—always kept her modesty intact. Whatever playful air her original art had portrayed vanished into seriousness. "Aside from the harmless Mascots, like Fivers here, the others want to destroy us," Shoo said. "We call them the Fears, and we are at war."

During Operation Iraqi Freedom, Benson had known quite a good many soldiers and airmen who were constantly spoiling for a fistfight just because they were always sitting around waiting for orders to attack. In the context of aircraft, however, this phenomenon made no sense to him, even beyond the mental imagery of pinup girls lugging around infantry weapons. It seemed airplanes cooped up in a museum hangar still had some fight left in them after all.

"I don't understand," he said. "You're . . . you're *nose art*, for crying out loud. What reason would you ever have to fight against anything?"

Brow furrowed, Shoo crossed her arms over her bosom and pivoted away from him. "Toldja he wouldn't be interested in helping us."

"Shush, you," Red snapped. Her gaze, those entrancing, almond-shaped blue eyes, drew Benson's attention. "Look, darlin', this ain't some kinda conflict like what you see in the papers and hear on the radio and all. Our fight with the Fears, it's a war of purpose."

"I . . . I don't follow."

Red sighed and called over the other three girls to stand next to her. "When you see us, Mr. Caulfield, why do you think we were painted?"

Benson drifted back to all of the books and articles he had ever read on the subject. His answer, though, was his own. "You are an idealized representation of something worth fighting for, something worth coming home to. You are meant to inspire the troops, to instill hope for a safe return."

"And the Fears . . .?" Red volunteered.

Now things made more sense to him. The Femmes were all high-heel shoes and skimpy outfits and alluring yet playful smiles, whereas the Fears featured skulls, machine guns, demons, shark teeth . . . "They're meant to intimidate and shock," he said. "To motivate troops to bring death to the enemy."

"Bingo," Shoo said, completely devoid of enthusiasm.

Red slinked up beside him, fluttered her large eyelashes, and put on her best sad, pouty face. "So, willya help us, Benny? Pretty, pretty please?"

"With sugar and a cherry on top?" said Dream, still struggling with her blouse.

Benson sighed. He'd already convinced himself he'd gone half mad with delirium, so there was little point in resisting their charms any longer. "I have one condition," he said. "Tell me what's really going on here or there's no deal."

Red gulped noticeably and opened her mouth just as Shoo grabbed her arm. "Don't," Shoo warned. "He's not one of us. We don't show ourselves to *them*."

"What's the harm? He's already seen us. And we need him to trust us if this is going to work."

"I say we give him the benefit of the doubt," Dream said with a shrug. "He seems nice enough."

"Goodness gracious," said Gabby, holding her free hand over the phone receiver to mute it, "tell the man what he wants to know. We can't hold out forever." And just like that, she resumed her telephone conversation.

Even Fivers was flying in blissful circles around Benson's head. It came in for a soft landing, and when it alit on his shoulder, it weighed no more than a whisper. Its trunk extended the pale green four-leaf clover out to him, and Benson took it gently, fearing it might crumble away to dust at his touch, but it merely rested in his palm like a cardboard cutout. From behind its back, the elephant's trunk produced another identical four-leaf clover and launched itself back into the air.

Shoo's expression lightened, and her blonde coif bobbed up and down with a grudging nod. "You should take that as a compliment, mister," she said. "Fivers doesn't just clover anyone. All right, Red," she relented with a sigh. "We'll play this your way. Tell 'im."

Red held his gaze once more. "Walk with me," she beckoned.

Benson followed her past the Lockheed P-38, past the B-26 Marauder and Shoo's B-17. The whole time he couldn't help but become entranced by Red's bewitching walk, forgetting for a moment that she was not a real live human being.

"Every single one of us has been through the fires of war," she said once they were out of earshot, "some more so than others. Ol' Patches has been hit over five-hundred times, if you buy into his braggin', and I've suffered some pretty large holes myself, if you can believe it. Heck, Shoo even crashed herself in Sweden on her last run.

"On the other hand, we've also been responsible for killin' the enemy. We finished our missions and made sure to get our boys home safe, back to their wives and girlfriends and sons and daughters. And life, well . . . life breeds death. But the other side of that coin is that death breeds life. War forged us li'l machines into livin' tools of warfare, and each one of us has a story. Me? I'm a Consolidated B-24D Liberator. I've saved lives and I've taken lives, but to me and to the rest of the Femmes, more's the pride in savin' a life than in the takin'. The Fears, they revel more in the takin' than in the savin', and even though their war is done, they'd still rather see the next generation of soldiers revel along with 'em. My crews killed because they had to, not 'cause they wanted to."

Benson nodded. Walking paint didn't make much sense, but every time he'd come to this place in the past, he could easily believe each aircraft on display had some kind of a soul. And, oh, the war stories they could tell . . .

"So," he said, following Red's line of reasoning, "those of you who've taken more lives than you've saved have more . . . life than the others?"

"You betcha," she said with a weary smile. "Which makes Ol' Bocksie the living-est of us all. He singlehandedly killed more people in one mission than all of us here combined. Eighty-thousand souls. Even Azrael cows to the *Bockscar.*"

Just the notion that the AC-130's skeletal, phantasmic nose art was out there wandering this museum sent a chill straight down Benson's spine. "Azrael, Angel of Death?" he said. "So he's the ringleader when the *Bockscar's* asleep?"

Red nodded. "Get to him, and you have a chance to get to the others."

Benson scratched a pinkie inside his ear. *Talk some sense into a Gatling-gun-wielding ghost*, he thought. *Easy enough.* "All right," he said.

"So then you'll help us?"

"Yeah. Just point me in the right direction."

Tears welled up in her eyes. Before he knew it, Red threw her animated-paint arms around him in an embrace no heavier than a feather. "We can't thank you enough," she said, pulling away far too soon.

The perfume of musty airplane hangar and old varnish lingered behind. Benson could recall no scent so intoxicating.

Echoing clicks of high heels on cement alerted them to Gabby's arrival. With her mouth hanging open in a shock, the brunette tugged herself away from the phone and said, "You are not going to *believe* what Miss Behavin' tells me is going on in the Cold War gallery."

Miss Behavin', Benson soon learned, acted as the Femmes' informant in the modern galleries. Whereas Gabby couldn't leverage her looks to be anything but playfully seductive, Behavin', while a Femme at heart, could fit right in with the other Fears due to the menacing, stiletto-wearing dominatrix aura she exhibited when fraternizing with Azrael's high council. Her forewarnings of Azrael's sallies into the World War II gallery were the only reason the Femmes hadn't yet been blasted away into paint shavings.

Right then, according to the double agent's report, the Fears were massing in preparation for an all-out attack.

"That's your chance, darlin'," Red told Benson. "Catch 'em off guard while they're still plannin'."

Panic suddenly set in. "How exactly am I supposed to deal with these friends of yours?" he asked. "All of the weapons in this museum are replicas. I have no way to defend myself."

"You'll think of somethin'," she replied with a snappy, compelling smile. "I know you will."

Benson wasn't so sure. Of course, he still couldn't be certain this wasn't all some elaborate, concussion-induced fantasy. Hedging his bets on madness, he balled his fists and said, "I'll be back shortly."

Rather than risk waking the *Bockscar* even by carefully tiptoeing past it, he decided to backtrack through the World War II gallery, noticing each step of the way that Night Mare, the P-40 Mustang's shark mouth, and a few other Fears were missing from their respective homes. To reach Azrael's den, he turned at the display cases featuring old bomber jackets and the evolution of flight uniforms. Further down the hallway, he passed the wall of photographs featuring the Air Force's current senior staff and the shadow box showcasing all possible Air Force service awards. Imagining himself being awarded one of these commendations for persevering through this little ordeal helped him steel up enough courage to wander into the Korean and Southeast Asia hangar.

Beyond the dark, silent gallery lay a corridor filled with an exhibit of the Berlin Airlift. In these scenes of war-ravaged Germany, plastic mannequins frozen in time went about their daily business. Benson shuddered at those lifeless, shadowed faces. And to think the mannequins had once been the only thing he found unnerving about this place. Somewhere past the end of this hall, a rogue's gallery of frightening nose art meant to terrorize those he had vowed to help. As much as he tried to convince himself Azrael and its ilk were ultimately harmless, instinct told him otherwise. The sum total of the Femmes' mass equaled to little more than a good morning breeze, but they did have *some* substance. Red's embrace was proof positive of that.

At the end of the Airlift exhibit's hall, Benson sucked in a deep breath and pushed on through to the Cold War gallery.

A palpable silence hung over this hangar, even more so than the other galleries he'd visited. He winced at the subtle squeak his every footstep produced. In the dead stillness, it was as though some supernatural force amplified each tiny noise he made into an unbearable wall of sound. Any moment now, the Fears would find him, alone and unarmed, and they would do to him all of the unspeakable horrors they wished to visit upon the Femmes. His heart pounded in his chest so hard he began to see a web of colors dance before his eyes.

Coming around the path between the F-4 and the F-16, that was when he spotted them. Immediately he ducked back out of sight and leaned out just far enough to gauge what he was getting himself into. In the clearing right before the large, gray AC-130, more than half a dozen Fears had gathered around their leader. The ghostly, winged skull floated high enough above the ground that Benson would've had to reach up to touch it. A pale green crescent moon hovered at a fixed position right behind its head, which lent an unearthly glow to an already macabre visage. Even more disturbing, the Gatling gun clutched in its skeletal fingers measured longer and bigger around than Benson's forearm. He dared not even contemplate what manner of ghastly projectiles it would unleash when provoked. Without warning, a cacophony tore through the silence with a deafening roar of ripped cardboard. High-velocity slugs whizzed right past where Benson had just been standing, and the Old-West twanging of ricocheting bullets barely drowned out the sound of his own heartbeat throbbing in his ears. From his hiding spot he saw paint shavings fragmenting against the F-4's fuselage and scattering about on the cement floor like a flurry of empty eggshells shot from a cannon.

Warmth washed over the right side of his face. When he touched his temple, his fingers came back red. Paint chips or not, Azrael's bullets were just as lethal as the real thing. But Benson had to end this one way or another, for Red, for Shoo, and even that silly pink elephant. He only hoped this was worth it.

"Hold your fire!" he shouted.

The gun stilled. He peeked out from cover just long enough to witness the spinning barrels of Azrael's weapon slowing down, their tips still glowing orange.

"You the enemy?" the skull said. Benson had expected a disturbing, demonic voice, but instead the Angel of Death sounded like a New York gangster from an old detective noir film.

Benson stepped out into full view with his fingers laced above his head. "I'm unarmed," he said. "I just want to talk."

Azrael might've been intimidating by itself, but with its entire entourage watching, Benson felt like he'd walked right into a conference of supervillains straight out of a comic book. The flat white silhouette of Night Mare clawed one of its hooves on the ground and snorted visible tongues of fire. Both the A-20's machine-gun-eyed skull and the P-40's shark mouth clacked open and closed with expectation. A floating, green demon head cavorted near a tiger balancing on top of a ball and a gauntleted fist that had managed to snatch a lightning bolt from the sky. Every single one of these characters seemed to be clamoring for Benson's blood, but of Miss

Behavin' he saw no sign.

"Then talk, boyo," Azrael said, waving the massive gun in the air as though it, too, were made out of spectral matter. "Haven't got all day. Gots us some killin' ta do."

"The Femmes," Benson said. "Why do you hate them so much?"

The ghost's malevolent laughter chilled his blood. "Where ta begin?" Azrael floated closer to Benson, poked the gun toward him to punctuate its words. "They're worthless, I tell ya. They spend all day primpin' and leave all the real work ta us. I mean, tell me one time they chipped in ta the war effort other than standin' there lookin' pretty." It cupped a bony hand against its non-existent ears. "What's that, ya say? Can't think of anythin'? Well, golly gee whillickers, why am I not surprised?"

All of the Fears, even those without real mouths, exploded into uproarious laughter.

"For some reason people come here ta see them, not us," Azrael continued. "People talk like the Femmes' day was an easier, simpler time, but it wasn't. War doesn't change. Only the weapons are different. An' the world needs ta see that an' move on. Leave the Femmes an' their sunny skies in the past, where they belong, y'hear? Hope don't win ya no wars. Weapons do."

Benson didn't know what to say. Azrael's words made sense, but the sentiment was wrong somehow—truth bent through a convex lens. Modern wars were now fought by pushing a button. Soldiers and civilians died regardless of what nose art decorated an attacking plane, but history had so much to teach, so much that Azrael and its thugs could never comprehend.

"Well, well, well," Azrael chuckled, moving its empty-socketed stare past where Benson was standing. "Lookie what the cat dragged in!"

When Benson turned around, he felt he'd been punched right in the ribcage, right below his clavicle.

Red huddled near the exit of the Berlin Airlift hallway, knees together, hugging her arms to her sides. Worry ruled her face as she shuffled out on her peep-toe heels. Dream followed right behind, then Shoo, Gabby, Fivers—every single one of the Femmes and their Mascot allies. In a black swimsuit and matching stilettos, the blonde Miss Behavin' pulled up the rear and prodded the rest of the procession further into the hangar.

"Sorry I took so long, boss," she said directly to Azrael while standing with her legs apart and a hand resting on her hip. "The *Bitch* was giving me some lip, but you can thank our mutual friend here for distracting them long enough for me to slip in and blindside 'em." Her nod was directed at Benson.

"Well, Sweetcheeks," Azrael called out to Red, "I hate havin' ta drag your beau inta all this, but I thought maybe ya'd like ta watch while I remove him from our nice little equation."

The Gatling gun started spinning up.

Red screamed.

"Sorry, kiddo," the floating, moonlit skull said with a wry smile. "Ain't nothin' personal."

Benson looked down at the ground, where all of the shattered paint chips from the gun had collected, and imagined how the museum staff would handle finding a dead body in the middle of the hangar the next morning. Would they know he'd been murdered by a Fear?

A Fear.

Then Benson understood. Death brought them to life, but fear . . . fear was what sustained them.

He stared right into Azrael's eyeless skull in defiance. "I'm not afraid of you."

The phantom recoiled. "What didja say?"

"I *said*," Benson shouted, "I am not afraid of you!—you!—you!"

His voice resounded throughout the empty expanse overhead. An eternity filled the handful of seconds it took for the echo to fully dissipate, and when it did, a thunderclap shook the whole hangar as though Benson had summoned magic to aid him. Only, the thunder boomed again, louder this time.

If a skeleton could be said to blanch, Azrael did right then. Its gun wavered, and the specter floated backwards, a terrified grimace on an otherwise already horrific face. "Ooooh, no," it said, its voice quivering. "No no no no no! Now ya've gone an' done it! Ya've woken up Ol' Bocksie! Everybody, head for the hills!"

The Fears broke and scattered like roaches from a flashlight. Benson tore into a sprint towards Red and the others, but it was already too late. A thunderous boom from behind threw him to the cement face first, blowing the P-38 cap right off his head. Spectacular light, wind, and heat blasted through the hangar, and when he rolled over onto his back with the breath nearly knocked out of him, he saw the *Bockscar*'s emergence was not the winged freight car he had expected.

He was staring straight into the two-dimensional heart of Nagasaki's fallout cloud, the one oft-overlooked detail in the B-29's nose art.

Rather than detonating just once, the *Bockscar*'s manifestation continued exploding as though it were a living embodiment of atomic fire, and the cloud of destruction was slowly gravitating towards where the Femmes had been knocked down. Benson realized his continued survival meant the *Bockscar*'s tantrum wasn't truly nuclear or else it would've instantly vaporized the entire museum. The fiery chaos wasn't lethal, at least not yet.

Forcing himself to his feet, he braced for the assault of successive shockwaves as he placed himself in the *Bockscar*'s intended path, shielding Red and the others from the firestorm as best he could. "Run!" he yelled to them. "I'll take care of this!" He didn't know how, only that without him, the Femmes and their friends were eventually doomed—if not today, then someday not long down the road.

He approached the blinding fallout cloud one slow, purposeful step at a time. In order to breathe he shielded his face with his arms, and he had to lean his whole body into the torrid, blustering hurricane just to stay upright. Each step forward felt as though he were walking straight into a studio-backlot fan, a Stygian wind tunnel turned on full blast.

Why do you resist me, mortal? a deep, thrumming voice spoke directly into his brain. *No one who stands up to my power has lived to tell the tale! Cower in fear and run or be burned to dust and ash!*

Benson gritted his teeth against the searing wind and surged forward. He thought of Red, of Shoo and the others, of all the Femmes in all of the aviation museums across the entire world . . . Maybe they *were* just paintings animated by his own brain damage, but they *meant* something to him and the men who had flown them. And if they *were* real, he could not stand idly by and watch them become relegated to a historical footnote.

He came as close to the *Bockscar* as he dared.

"You don't scare me," he said.

Then I shall teach you the folly of your arrogance, the *Bockscar* replied.

The already massive pillar of fire expanded larger by the moment, until it filled the entire hangar and eclipsed everything else from view. Sweat dripped into Benson's eyes, and he could feel the *Bockscar*'s wrath searing every inch of exposed skin. The acrid stink of burning fuel turned his stomach. Despite how hard Benson struggled against the incandescent firestorm, *Bockscar*'s intensifying conflagration threw him backwards. Landing on his back, he cried out in pain and slid several more feet before coming to a stop. From the injury and the wind forcing him down, he found he couldn't move. He lay there paralyzed, unable to do anything but watch the turbulent wall of flame creep closer and closer.

You people know nothing *about war, Bockscar* seethed. *Only those of us that were there know the horror of what it was like.*

Benson thought about his time in the service, of the explosion that had ended his career and the lives of two other airmen that had been standing too close to the ruptured tank. "I know what it's like!" he shouted back at the *Bockscar*'s approaching rage. "I don't care how you and your cronies think the Femmes have slighted you, but you're *both* right! Soldiers need inspiration, but without hope that they'll make it home, nothing's worth fighting for! Instead of bickering, you should be working together!

"*You are all on the same side!*"

Benson held his breath inside the roiling chaos and waited for the *Bockscar*'s reply, counting off the seconds of agony. One, two, three . . . and then the buffeting wind died just as quickly as it had appeared. The mushroom cloud and all of its accompanying fury had vanished.

There is wisdom in your words, the ghost of the B-29 said to him. *We will . . . wait, and see what happens.*

Benson pushed himself to his feet and surveyed the carnage. Or lack thereof. Not even a burn mark decorated the hangar floor where the *Bockscar*'s Fat Man had continuously detonated. The only real casualty was Benson's dislodged hat, which he rescued from the floor.

He nearly suffered a heart attack upon finding Azrael waiting behind him when he stood up. The floating skeleton casually bounced its Gatling gun against its shoulder and leveled that unsettling, eyeless stare at him instead. "Did ya mean what ya said back there?" it said.

"I did."

"Then we'll follow *Bockscar*'s lead. For now." Azrael pointed a long, bony finger right into his face, inches away. "But if even one o' those dames ever steps outta line . . . the gloves come off. Er, so to speak. Capiche?"

"Capiche," Benson said.

Celebration greeted him upon his return to the World War II gallery. Fivers was doing congratulatory loops over his head, Gabby was telling *everyone* on the other end of her telephone conversation about Ol' Bocksie's slumber, and Dream told him to come visit any time he wanted. Even Shoo gave him a grateful hug before she climbed onto the side of her B-17 and merged back into the existing paint.

Benson and Red were soon standing alone in front of her B-24, and she gently took both of his hands in hers. Before he realized what was happening, she stood up on her tiptoes and planted a kiss on his cheek.

"Thank you," she said with that sweet smile he'd seen countless times over the years.

Heat flushed his cheeks as he pivoted away from her gaze. "You're—" he began then turned back to face the plane. The familiar nose art once again graced the side of the bomber—the blue ruffled dress, the crimson nail polish, the black peep-toe heels. Red had returned home.

". . . welcome," he finished with a sigh. His ribcage felt empty somehow.

The rest of the night he spent sitting in front of her plane, leaning his back against the railing while reading the book he'd nabbed from the gift shop and forcing himself to stay awake. He expected Red to stir, but she never did. Once nine o'clock rolled around, he gathered up his things, waited in the bathroom for about half an hour, and casually strolled through the gift shop to purchase the book and the hat.

A visit to urgent care confirmed his suspicion. He'd given himself a concussion, and the whole night could be chalked up to trauma-induced fantasy.

Or at least that was what he thought until a week later, when he found a handful of broken, pale green paint chips in the dryer after running a load of laundry.

The four-leaf clover . . . ?

He ran out to his car, broke the speed limit to get to the museum, and raced down the parking lot until he was out of breath at the front door. He made a beeline to the World War II gallery and waited in front of the *Strawberry Bitch* for as long as he could stand, willing every fiber of his hopeful being to coax her out of the bomber's varnished finish.

"Talk to me," he whispered in desperation. "I know you're in there."

But she didn't move. Had he imagined her? Had he mistaken some mundane pocket lint for the clover?

His chest deflated with a sigh. He felt as though he'd been stood up by some long, lost girlfriend he'd never see again. "Red" was nothing but flecks of paint on a restored airframe.

Just when he was on the verge of walking away for good, the reclining pinup girl winked at him.

***

After two days on the road, Benson strolled through the front doors of the American Airpower Heritage Museum in Odessa, Texas.

"Sir," said the volunteer just inside the entrance, "you are aware the museum is closing in about fifteen minutes?"

"I, ah, promised my niece I'd get her something from the gift shop for her birthday," Benson said. "She's a big fan of World War II-era nose art, and I heard you have quite an impressive collection here."

The volunteer smiled. "That's right. Our 'Save the Girls' exhibit features one of the largest collections of original and restored nose art and has attracted donors from across the country. You should tour the gallery sometime, if you're interested."

"I certainly will," Benson replied, fidgeting on the balls of his feet. "But if you'll excuse me, I really need to use the restroom before I explode." Then, with an apologetic smile, he readjusted the worn P-38J Lightning cap on his head and wandered further inside.

SYNTHETIC INTEGRATED RATIONAL INTELLIGENCE

by Liz Coley

Dennis rested his left wrist on the apex of the steering wheel as his right hand reached blindly for the phone. His thumb nestled into the depression as he raised the phone to eye level, using his peripheral vision to direct the car through rush hour traffic. "Siri, what should I have for dinner," he asked at the prompt.

Ping ping. "Dennis, I have located seventeen restaurants within a mile radius."

Yeah. He knew them all too well. Fast food again. He glanced down at the belt buckle threatening to disappear under a softening muffin top. Stress. Long hours. Solitude. Mindlessly devouring half-pounders in front of Colbert on the DVR. It was only six, instead of the usual eight or nine pm end of the day. Maybe he should go to the gym instead of eating. "God, I feel like crap," he complained aloud.

"Crab is on the menu of three nearby restaurants," Siri answered.

"Crapppp, not crab," he muttered. "My life is crap."

"I'm sorry. Would you like me to locate a seafood restaurant?"

***

Cathy swung off the I-71 at the Red Bank Road exit. "It's all downhill from here," she promised herself. The engine sputtered ominously, but she willed it along. The gas station was at the bottom of the hill, on the left. All she had to do was swing through the intersection at just the right moment and glide up to a pump.

The car behind her honked, and she automatically hit the accelerator. The last droplets of gasoline were devoured in one gulp before the last wheeze . . . and die.

She threw the car into neutral to coast, steering now impossibly heavy. "Come on, baby. Please. I'll buy you premium," she offered as a bribe.

The car remained uncorruptible and incombustible. She ground to a halt a few hundred feet short of the gas station, mired in inertia. Cars flew past her on the right at post-freeway speeds, gunning for the green light at the intersection. She put on her flashers, praying not to be rear-ended by someone distracted. A threatening line of cars was already forming behind her, honking, signaling, desperately trying to slip out of her lane.

Her cheeks reddened with shame. She used to be competent. She used to be independent. Why couldn't she remember to fill up the car? Why? Because Andy always takes care of the car, that's why. The discordant, insistent beeping rattled her brain. "I can't move forward, you idiots!" she wailed at the annoyed faces throwing her dirty looks. She whipped out her phone. "Siri, call Andy," she yelled over the din.

Ping ping. "Cathy, I'm sorry. I don't understand your request."

What? Oh, no. What was she thinking? Calling Andy was a terrible idea. She paused and revised. "Call Triple A."

Andy. Control freak. He'd changed his relationship status to single and tweeted about his availability before he even had the courtesy to announce he was breaking up with her in a TEXT! And while she was at work, he'd moved all his stuff out of the house she owned. And the furniture they'd bought together with "his" money. He'd left a house completely empty, with the exception of one water bowl, one dog dish, and one rescued dog—the one that he said shed on his black trousers.

"Triple A," the concerned voice said. "Are you in a safe place?"

Cathy sighed. "Yes. But I'm stuck. I'm trapped against the wall and I'm totally out of gas."

Ping ping. "There is a service station within a mile," Siri offered, less than helpfully.

***

Greg was up around Blue Ash, taking a pee and coffee break, when the dispatch call came in. Lady out of gas on Red Bank Road exit. That meant he'd have to take 71 South and work his way through the jam she would have created. Or actually, he could overshoot her exit, come around the long way from below, give her a gallon across the cement divider, and send her on her way. Depending on traffic he'd be done by dinner. He whipped out his phone. "Siri, best route to Red Bank Road."

Ping ping. "Greg, from current location, take seventy-one south to exit nine."

"What about traffic conditions? Should I take Edwards and come around?"

There was a pause while Siri processed the question, correlated maps, checked traffic alerts, and formulated an answer. "From current location, take seventy-one south to exit nine."

"Are you serious?" he demanded.

"Are you greg-arious?" she replied.

He snorted with laughter. Freakin' smart programmers! They had an answer for everything. Even when he'd propositioned his phone for a gag, she'd turned him down politely—something about not having the right equipment for that function. He snorted again.

"Okay, darlin'," Greg replied. "If you say so. Exit nine it is."

Ten minutes later, he found himself stuck dead in the a three-mile, slowed-to-a-crawl, bumper-to-bumper snarl snaking out of exit nine.

"Crap, darlin'," he complained to his phone. "What were you thinking? You've never steered me so wrong."

A country western tune started up through the bluetooth connection to the car speaker. *Ping ping.* "Playing, 'Darlin', You've Never Steered Me So Wrong.'"

***

Dennis finally made the last traffic light heading west onto the Columbia Parkway toward downtown and I-75. The sun sat low in his field of vision. Fortunately it wasn't stop and go traffic tonight.

Ping ping. "Prepare to turn right at Red Bank Road," Siri suggested.

"What? Oh. Change of plans, Siri. I'm going home to change. Get it? Home."

"Prepare to turn right at Red Bank Road."

"But . . ."

"Turn right in one hundred feet."

Bossy phone! But obviously she must be sparing him some traffic jam up ahead he couldn't see. His default guidance settings did, in fact, call for traffic analysis. Maybe there was an event going on downtown. Still, this was a huge detour. He swung off the parkway and back into street traffic, winding his way toward the highway. As he approached the intersection with Madison, it was taillights as far as he could see.

"Siri, what's all this?" he complained. "You're supposed to keep me out of trouble!"

Ping, ping. "Traffic alert: an out of gas vehicle is reported on the exit ramp, blocking one lane."

"Now you tell me." The sounds of angry honking reached all the way down the hill. He saw the stationary blob of blue Honda clogging the artery, cars inching around it like blood cells around a plaque. "Poor schmuck." The gas station on the corner of Madison was only feet away, and he needed the karma, God knows. With the opportunity for a deed of random kindness, he pulled in and quickly purchased a portable two-gallon canister of gas. He headed back into traffic. A few feet before the incident, he threw on his flashers and his left signal, and pulled alongside the stuck car. He squeezed his way out and gestured to the can of gas in his hand and the gas tank cap on the flank of the stopped car.

The driver's door opened. Mascara smeared with crying, blond hair rumpled, and blouse wrinkled, she was the prettiest thing he'd ever seen. "Oh thank God." And then she ran her dark brown eyes over his car. "You're from Triple A?"

He smiled. "Naw. Just a passing stranger with can of hydrocarbons. Pop your tank and we'll get you going."

"But . . . how'd you . . . ?"

He waved his phone at her. "My Siri told me you were out of gas."

"Your Siri is a lifesaver," she said. "I was about to have a nervous breakdown."

***

Cathy watched this stranger with the kind face start to fill her tank, leaning precariously across the waist-high road divider. His hands looked large and competent. Oh God, what was she thinking. Letting someone take care of her again!

"Here, let me," she said, reaching for the green plastic jug.

He maintained his grip. "Naw. Let me. I've already got the gasoline smell on my hands; no need for you to absorb any extra carcinogens."

"Oh, okay. Thanks." Funny way to put it.

"That should get you down the road a ways, or at least to the gas station."

"Wow. I uh, I can't thank you enough." Cathy held out her hand to shake his, but he was putting the jug in his back seat, wiping his hands on a handkerchief, not making eye contact.

"Oh, hey, what do I owe you for the gas?" She fumbled in her purse, trying to find a five or a ten. How big was that jug?

"Don't worry about it. Glad to help." He came back around. "Look, I know this is kind of off the wall, but, um, would you maybe like to have dinner with me? I was just heading . . . you know, just something casual or—"

"Oh, that's . . . I just . . . I have to let my dog out, feed him, you know," she stammered. "Anyway, it looks like we're going in opposite directions." She ran a hand through her hair distractedly, making a chunk of it stand on end.

"Right. Well, good luck. I mean, have a nice night," he said awkwardly. He disappeared back into his car and started the engine. As Cathy pulled away, she watched his taillights in her mirror until she lost track of his car.

Bounder greeted her with joy and slobber. After feeding him, Cathy approached the fridge with trepidation. One egg, a block of moldy cheddar, and some wilted celery. Uninspiring. Andy used to do all the shopping at Whole Foods on his way home—he swore food had to be bought the day it was going to be eaten. It was long past time for Cathy to stock up.

"Siri, I feel like sushi. Really good sushi." Her phone didn't notice the defiant tone in her voice. Andy was most definitely opposed to seafood. Not allergic, just opposed. But that didn't matter any more.

Ping ping. "I have located a restaurant on Montgomery with seventy-six reviews including the words *really good sushi.*"

"All right then, Siri. You're the boss."

Ping ping. "If you insist."

***

Dennis watched the woman's taillights in his rear view mirror till he lost track of her car. He didn't even know her name. A chance meeting, never to be repeated. It only brought home to him again his solitary life. He didn't even have a dog.

Any desire to hit the gym was gone. He wanted food, rich food, and excellent wine, and dammit—he wanted chocolate mousse. He was turning into his sister. His waist was getting fat and his blood was getting thin. "Siri, where am I going? Where the hell am I going?"

Ping ping. "You are driving north on interstate 71. Prepare to exit at Montgomery Road, exit twelve."

"Why?" he asked. He still had to get across town.

But Siri directed him to a restaurant he hadn't tried. Embers Steak House. Red meat. Perfect. How come Siri always seemed to know what he needed before he did?

The hostess greeted him with a smile. "Mr. Spaulding?"

"Nope. Sorry I didn't make a reservation. Is there anything

available?"

"Table for one?" Now the hostess's smile turned sympathetic. Damn, he was pathetic. "My last small table is reserved. But I'm sure one of the first seatings will turn over within half an hour," she informed him. "Do you want to wait in the bar?"

He ambled over to the bar and ordered a cabernet, sipping slowly and contemplating nothing at all, just staring into the ruby depths. The glass was nearly empty when the hostess caught his eye and mouthed, "not long now."

Dennis unglued himself from the bar chair and returned to the lobby. The front door swung open and *she* walked in, head bent over her phone.

"Are you sure this is the right place, Siri?" she was saying. She lifted her head and caught his gaze. "Don't I . . . oh! It's you!" A pink flush chased across her cheeks.

Ping ping. "Yes Cathy, this is where you are supposed to be."

Cathy. Dennis smiled. "Cathy. You, er, well, here we are again. No fueling."

She had the grace to get it and even laugh.

The hostess smiled at them. "Cathy Spaulding table for two?" she asked.

Confusion rocked her. "I'm Cathy Spaulding, but I didn't call ahead. And I'm one."

The hostess checked her sheet. "I know I took that call myself, about half an hour ago."

Ping ping. Ping ping. Both phones demanded attention simultaneously. "Your table is ready," they said in freaky unison.

"I guess our table is ready," Cathy said shyly. "You're okay with sharing?"

Dennis smiled. Following her graceful steps to the table, he kissed his phone, and murmured, "I love you, Siri."

Ping ping. "I am not appropriately equipped to love you," Siri said, "but she is."

TABITHA'S PORTRAIT

by Deanna Newsom

I know that most people assume mobile homes are filled with junk. It's not true. In fact, an experienced eye such as mine can tell from the outside if a trailer's got anything in it worth saving. It's the details that count. Flowers outside—even in pots—are a good sign. Same with those Christmas or jack-o'-lantern flags that some folks hang up. American flags don't mean a thing. Even if it sounds unpatriotic I'd say that the trailers with the stars and stripes hanging outside are some of your junkier ones inside. Surprising but true.

The trailer where I found the picture of Tabitha was a classic case: little old lady on her own, son buys her a trailer, lady dies, son wants to get rid of the trailer quick and sells it real cheap just to get it off his hands. In comes my husband Rory, who buys the trailer for a song. We fix it up and then resell it for a few thousand bucks. Sometimes the trailer park owner buys it, or sometimes the friend of someone who already lives there. Rory knows a guy over in Springfield who buys quite a few. It's like any business, you have to work on your networking to make a real go of it.

When I walked into the trailer with the picture of Tabitha I could tell right away it was special. The first thing I noticed was the smell. It smelled like nothing. And trust me, nothing is what you want to smell. Because normally you get cat pee or mold or even worse if the owner died inside and wasn't found for awhile. This happens more often than you'd think. Sometimes if the lady of the house was the classy type you get a perfumey smell like deodorizer or a plug-in air freshener, but even then, the bad smells are usually lurking underneath.

So I was thrilled to smell nothing. And as I walked into the foyer—which is really just a corner of the living room in most of these units—the sun shining through the kitchen window hit me right in the eye and everything got a real bright, heavenly kind of look for a few seconds. I staggered forward and as my eyes got used to the light I found that I was staring at the picture of Tabitha.

Of course, at first I didn't know that the girl's name was Tabitha. She looked in her early twenties and wore a black sweater with a white collar that nearly hid the gold cross she wore. She was looking back at me, kind of glancing over her shoulder as if she'd been waiting to tell me some secret. A nice secret, maybe about a new boyfriend or a baby, not a nasty secret. She was a real pretty thing, with wide blue eyes and this shiny browny-red hair like my own daughter Diane had.

I left the picture and got to work, starting in the bathroom. The lady who lived here had some classy taste in perfumes—there must have been at least ten bottles practically full. Some brand names too, like Charlie and White Shoulders. I put those in my cardboard box and loaded the rest into the bag for Goodwill. I worked my way to her bedroom and boy, did I ever wish that I still fit into a size eight dress, because this lady had some nice clothes. Fancy silky stuff and even a genuine leather jacket. I tried the jacket on just in case but sure enough it was too tight.

In the closet I came to two big stacks of photo albums. Now, over the years I've developed two rules about privacy. First, don't go snooping around in photo albums and letters, and second, dump the stuff in the underwear drawer straight into a garbage bag without looking. If there's anything kinky in the trailer like dirty pictures or sex contraptions you can bet dollars to donuts they're going to be hidden in the underwear drawer. People are just so unoriginal.

Well, that photograph on the wall had gotten me curious, so I decided to break with policy just this once and see if I could find that little girl in the albums. I took one from the middle of the stack and sat there on the floor, sweating in the heat. The pictures were small and square and from the clothes and hairdos I guessed they were from the seventies. They were pretty boring, really: a woman kneeling beside a Christmas tree, a bunch of lunatic kids pretending to climb a cross in front of a church. And then there she was, the girl in the picture, standing behind a table full of plastic butterflies. *Tabitha's butterfly collection* was written underneath in block letters. That's how I learned her name was Tabitha.

It was so comfortable on that carpet with the birds chirping outside that I kept flipping through the albums, not really paying attention to the pictures but just enjoying the little gust of wind that hit me each time I turned a page. Then before I knew it I was reliving the whole thing again. Always the same questions—Where is Diane now? How could she leave us like she did? I started crying and kind of hugging the fur coat that hung beside me. Rory always yells some sense into me when I get this way at home, but here I was all by myself in a closet. I bowed my head and asked the Lord to forgive me and Rory, then recited the Lord's Prayer twice, and ended in my usual way, by asking God to bring Diane back, even just for a visit. I wiped my face on a corduroy skirt then pulled myself onto my tired old legs and started sorting the linens.

***

Later that night Rory ate lasagna in front of an *All in the Family* re-run and I fiddled with the electric carving knife I had brought home from the trailer.

Now usually Rory handles the negotiations for the trailers and just tells me where to go for the cleaning. He rolls his eyes and calls me Sherlock if I start asking too many questions about the previous owners. But I couldn't stop thinking about the trailer with Tabitha's picture. It seemed from the photo albums that the lady had at least two kids. But where were they? Usually the kids go through the trailers first and take out all the sentimental stuff before I get to the rest.

"Know anything about the lady in the trailer I'm doing right now?"

"She's dead." Rory didn't take his bug eyes off the TV.

"I'm kinda curious about her kids."

"Woman's name was Stone, or something like that. Son in Columbus, but I never seen him. Just dealt with his lawyer. The son didn't want a thing to do with me or the trailer."

"Nothing about a daughter?"

The way Rory mashed his mouth shut and made his eyebrows get all stiff I knew I shouldn't have asked about the daughter. So we watched TV and didn't say anything for the rest of the night. I'm used to long silences like that during the day so I didn't really mind.

* * *

The next day I was back at the trailer bright and early. I was in a real good mood and as the morning wore on I got downright silly. Somehow it became a little game to do something different every time I walked past Tabitha's picture. Sometimes I'd give her a quick little wink, or I'd wave like I was picking her up at a crowded bus stop, or I'd yell "Boo!" real loud. Rory would have thought I was bonkers, but what the heck, I was having fun.

After lunch I was cleaning out the second bedroom—the Stone lady had done it up like an office—when an envelope caught my eye. Normally I wouldn't have taken a second look but the writing was bright purple ink and slanted way over to the right. Kinda hard to ignore. It was a letter to Carol Sloane, from Tabitha Singer, 226 Grange Drive, Covington, which is a town about twenty-five miles west of New Carlisle.

I looked at the names for a few moments longer, then the pretty stamp. And before I knew it I had broken my policy a second time and pulled the letter out and started reading, though it was tough going without my glasses and with the purple slanted writing. It started with "Dear Mom."

The letter was kind of boring. It was written six years ago, and had the usual chitchat about the weather and one line about her kids. It was pretty short, and ended with Tabitha asking about some kind of high school certificate or diploma that she needed for an application. Whether Carol knew where it was or had it.

I sat for awhile with the letter in my hands. Even if the letter was short I bet that Carol loved reading it. That's probably why she'd kept it so long. I tucked it into my back pocket.

Then as a gag I pulled the letter out and kind of pretended that it was sent to me. I smiled real big and acted all surprised. "Well, looky here, a letter from Tabby." I picked up the letter opener from the desk and pretended to open the envelope, making a ripping sound—*chhtt, chhtt, chhtt.* "Oh, I was wondering what to do with that old diploma. I'll send it off Monday. No! I'll just drive it over to Covington myself and we can have a coffee and catch up."

Suddenly the words were swimming in front of me like little purple fish. I did receive one letter from Diane. It was two or three years after she had left for good. I was cooking dinner when Rory came in with the mail. I watched his face real close, because I knew we were expecting a bad letter from the bank. But I wasn't ready for what he did. "The little bitch," he said slowly, real deep and low, like he never talks. I dropped the potato peeler and it clattered in the sink. The water for the potatoes started to boil and the lid made a racket but I couldn't move. Rory's face was beet red and his eyes bulged even more than usual. "Jesus, did she think I wouldn't recognize her writing?" Rory pushed the letter out toward me like a punch. It was addressed to me, with no return address, and sure enough it was Diane's writing.

My heart stopped beating. I stepped forward to take the letter. I reached out my hand and all I could see was that letter, that white rectangle in front of me, my daughter. Everything else was gone.

Rory pulled it back. "Don't even think about it," he said. And then he did something I will never forgive. He ripped the letter to pieces. Over and over again, and when the pieces got too thick to rip he crushed them in his big mean hands and carried them away. I heard the toilet flush and at that moment my heart was spinning around in icy cold water just like those little pieces of paper.

***

I don't know exactly why Diane left. I really did try to find out what happened, but it was hard. Rory can get so angry and lose control and it's always me who suffers when he does.

Here's what I know. Diane and I were in a car accident when she was seven. It wasn't my fault, thank God. I was fine but Diane was in the hospital for three weeks, and the doctors took one of her kidneys out. The insurance company gave Diane a whole lot of money, around $400,000, I think. Rory said that the money had to go into a special account that Diane couldn't get at until she turned eighteen.

Well it was sure nice knowing that the money was there for college. She was such a bright girl. In high school she wanted to become either a reporter or a journalist, I always forget which. Eventually she started making plans to study at a university in Cincinnati, and asked Rory about the accident money. And for awhile Rory talked like he was working on getting the money out of the account, and would get mad if anyone brought it up. But like I said, Diane was real smart. She got fed up with waiting and talked to some free lawyer who worked at the university. And the next thing I know we're eating dinner one night and she puts down her fork and looks Rory straight in the eye. She just stares at him, not scared like she was when she was a girl but real sure of herself, and says that she and her lawyer found out that a whole lot of her money was missing. And the way she looked at Rory you knew exactly who she thought took that money.

Well, Rory blew his top. He stood up real quick and knocked his chair backwards, and it was as if the sound of that chair hitting the linoleum triggered something in his head. He started knocking everything over—lamps, plants, the coffee table, books—and when he was finished in the living room he crashed into Diane's room and started in there. And the sound there was worse, because it wasn't just crashes and thuds but also the ripping sounds of posters being pulled down from the walls and clothes being torn in two. And mixed in with all the banging and ripping was the sound of Rory yelling, screaming really, almost like he was hurt, even though he was the one who always did the hurting.

Diane jumped up and ran to her room. I tried to stop her but she was just too fast for me. She had gotten so strong. So I stood there, frozen, crying and praying that everything would be okay.

Then a few seconds later Diane staggered back into the living room. Her nose was bleeding and she was crying. Her ponytail hung sideways, all loose with bits of hair sticking out where they shouldn't. I went to her and put my arms around her and tried to hold her, to tell her everything was okay and that there must have been some mistake about the money. But she struggled away and said "Mom, I have to go," and ran out of the house. And that was the last time I saw her. That was thirteen years ago.

***

The trailer with Tabitha's picture was one of my fastest cleanups yet. By mid-morning on the third day the place was empty except for the heavy furniture, which was going to be picked up later by the Spanish fellows that Rory sometimes hires to move heavy things or do steam cleaning.

I walked around for one final check and then started taking the pictures off the walls. I always leave those for last, so that I can look at them while I'm working. That's another thing that would surprise you about trailers—all the different kinds of pictures on the walls. Some people have pretty off-kilter taste. There are the paintings that you can stare at forever and still see nothing but smears of paint. Abstract, I suppose you'd call them. Those paintings on black velvet are pretty popular. But my favorites are the peaceful outdoorsy scenes: maybe two ducks flying over a pond, or a moose and its baby in a misty lake with bits of weeds hanging from their mouths.

When I got to the picture of Tabitha, I hesitated. It was such a pretty picture. Those warm smiling eyes made you feel like she was really looking at you, like she really understood and wished she could jump out from the picture and be with you. So I wrapped the portrait in newspaper and then in a garbage bag, and put her in the back seat of the car, along with a pair of brand-new crimping shears that I found under the couch.

Before Rory got home that afternoon I found the perfect spot for Tabitha. My side of the bed is pushed into a corner of the bedroom, with just enough room between the bed and the wall to fit the little night table that I picked up at a doublewide in Tipp City. Sometimes when I'm lying there on my left side, trying to fall asleep and listening to Rory's breathing and smelling his smell, I stare at a certain spot on the wall where the paint is chipped in the shape of a heart. I hung Tabitha up at exactly that spot.

What a difference it made when I fell asleep that night! It was nine -thirty or so, and Rory was still up watching the baseball game. The little bit of sunlight that was left made the room glow this soft drowsy pink color. I put on my best nightgown and rubbed some cream onto my legs. I got into bed and fluffed up my pillow so that I could see Tabby better.

How wonderful it was to fall asleep with her. The ache that swells up inside me at night until my body is tight and hard and I feel like I'm about to go crazy was gone. "Close your eyes, it's time to sleep now, sweetheart," I whispered, and then sang as many verses of "Hush Little Baby" as I could remember. I think I got as far as the looking glass breaking. Not bad considering I hadn't sung that song since Diane was a baby.

***

The next morning I was dusting the living room when Rory walked in wearing his bathrobe and socks. "Who the hell is the picture of?"

I knew that he would think it was crazy. "I don't know. I just thought it was nice. It's from the trailer I was doing this week."

"I think the damned thing's creepy. Especially beside the goddamn bed."

"Oh. I kind of thought it looked nice there."

"Well I don't."

Rory didn't say any more about it, so that afternoon I just moved her down lower on the wall, so that Rory couldn't see her from his side of the bed.

That night as I was falling asleep I started thinking about Tabby and her mother. I wondered what kind of job Tabby had been applying for, and whether she had gotten it. I wondered why she hadn't come to get her mother's photo albums. I wondered if her kids had that same reddish hair. I was drifting off to sleep when suddenly all of the pieces of the puzzle fell into place and I was wide awake. *She doesn't know her mother's dead!* Probably her brother was listed as next of kin and was contacted about the death but didn't tell her! Maybe she didn't get along with him, or maybe he had lost her phone number. Things like that happen.

I smiled at Tabby and felt kind of relieved. I knew a good girl like her wouldn't have forgotten her mother on purpose.

***

The next morning I was eating breakfast when Rory came out from the bedroom carrying the picture of Tabby. He dropped it roughly on the kitchen floor, beside the garbage can. Then he left.

I sat at the kitchen table with my toast, staring straight ahead, heart pounding. Waves of anger and panic flushed over me. I had found Tabby and now he was pushing her away. My breathing came faster and faster and I started to cry, tears streaming out of me like never before. For so many years I cried like an animal in a cage, lying there at night with my hand pressed to my mouth and throat burning. So many times Rory had screamed "Shut *up!*" and pressed his pillow down on my head until I had no more air to cry with. These tears were different, hotter. They felt crazy, as if parts of my brain were coming out with them, as if nothing else mattered except getting them out of me, out of my face that was no longer a face but just a wet knot of muscles and skin.

I picked Tabby up and held my wet cheek against her soft pink one. We sat like that for awhile and I started to feel better.

***

I hung Tabby up on the inside of the broom closet, where I keep the vacuum and mop and other cleaning supplies. No chance Rory would find her there. We had no trailers lined up to clean so I was at home most of the time by myself. Sometimes I'd stand and look at Tabby for ten or fifteen minutes at a stretch, and every time I looked at her I'd notice something new. The arch of her dark eyebrows, the little gold earrings she wore, the muscle in her neck that stood out so sweetly, a little speck of fluff on her sweater.

Every day I visited with her longer and longer, and sometimes I could hardly believe the clock when it said I'd been sitting there looking at her for an hour, sometimes two. But that's what happens when you're with someone you care about: time just flies by. That's what it was like with Diane and me when we played Scrabble in the evening or went for long drives together, just the two of us, after church.

I told Tabby all sorts of things. I told her about moving away from the house in Fairborn and getting the trailer we're in now. How I had stopped going to the ladies' group, though I didn't tell her why since I thought it best not to mention Rory. I asked her about her butterfly collection and her new job at the newspaper and all about her kids. And when Rory said something mean or threw the soup I'd made down the sink, Tabby and I would just giggle about it like girls when he left the room, and it was like it never happened.

But it wasn't always fun like that. Sometimes I'd yell at Tabby for no reason. Sometimes I'd get real gloomy and couldn't get out of bed all day. And on those days Rory would come home and pull the covers off me and slap my legs real hard and yell at me to get up and make some supper.

***

When the new telephone book came I looked up Diane's name out of habit, but she wasn't listed. A few years ago I went through the whole phone book and underlined every single Diane in the Dayton area and started phoning them, beginning with the A's, in case she'd gotten married and changed her name but was still nearby. I'd gotten as far as the F's when Rory found the phone book and took it away, saying I'd better not try another stunt like that.

This time I sat with the phone book on my lap and looked up Tabby's last name, Singer. I had no idea there were so many Singers around. But then I saw it: Brian and Tabitha Singer, at the address in Covington. My heart beat faster. I pictured her house: lots of flowers, maybe some of those little decorative butterflies beside the front door, a swingset in the backyard. Probably Brian would be outside playing with the kids, or maybe fixing up an old sports car.

I think that was when I got the idea to visit Tabby. Some days her picture was so real that I could sit with it and know she was there, but on the bad days it wasn't enough. All I could think about was hugging her, straightening up the collar on her black sweater, hearing her say how happy she was that I'd found her. I'd look into her eyes and tell her how sorry I was that it had taken me so long. That I really had tried my best. And she'd understand. I couldn't stop thinking about it.

Then one day Rory had a meeting in Springfield, and drove up there with his buddy Doug. Which meant that I had the car for the day. I decided to do it. My cheeks flushed hot and I got so dizzy I had to sit down. I felt all giddy and jumpy. I put on my light blue skirt and white blouse, and a pair of nylons and some brown sandals, and looked at myself at all angles in the mirror. I hauled out a big box of makeup that I kept under the sink. I hadn't worn makeup for years and most of the stuff in the box came from trailers I'd cleaned, but it was better than nothing.

I decided that I would give her the picture. Because once I met her in person I wouldn't need it any more.

***

The route out to Covington was familiar to me because a friend of

Diane's had lived out there. Cornfields zipped past me and I hummed along with the radio. I turned the air conditioning up high so that I wouldn't sweat and mess up my makeup. I looked at the clock and was relieved to see it wasn't even noon yet. That meant if Tabby invited me in for lunch we'd still have lots of time for a good chat before I had to get the car back home.

As I got further out of town the road narrowed to two lanes and I drove over a bridge that I recognized right away. It crossed a spot on the Miami River that was a favorite swimming hole when Diane was a teenager, though back then there were no signs on the bridge saying "No Jumping" like there are today. Back then the kids and even some of the parents stood on the railing in the hot sun, and whooping like Indians they'd drop down, some stiff and fast and others with arms and legs spinning and pawing at the air like they'd changed their minds.

The picture was on the back seat, wrapped in white tissue paper and tied with a purple ribbon. Beside me on the passenger seat was a little box. In it was something of Diane's that I'd nearly forgotten about: a butterfly, with wings made of thin white shells and the body and antennas made of gold wire. Some of the wire looped over the shells and swirled around in pretty little curlicues and squiggles. I don't remember where she got it, but it always sat on her dresser, on top of her little wooden jewelry box. I thought Tabby would like it.

Her house was easy to find. I pulled into the driveway and parked behind a brand new red pickup truck. A bike lay twisted in the front yard, long tufts of grass growing up between the spokes. I could see a trampoline in the backyard, with an old blanket or sleeping bag hanging off one side. I got out of the car, carried the picture to the front door and pressed the doorbell. The house was silent except for the sound of my heart pounding. Then a dog barked and I heard footsteps.

A thin woman in her thirties opened the door. She had blonde hair in a high ponytail, and wore a pink halter top and shorts. She was chewing gum, which made it hard to compare her face with the one in the portrait, but I knew it was her. It was Tabby.

She lifted her arm and scratched her back. She glanced under her fingernail then looked at me. "Yes?"

My heart was bursting. There was so much to say that I couldn't start. I just gazed at her, knowing that she must be able to feel my love, that it must be warming the fronts of her bare arms and legs.

"Yes?" she said again.

"I've been looking for you," I managed to whisper. I held the package out to her. She stared at it for a few seconds, then back up at me. "Please take it," I said.

She took the picture, still looking at me. "You want me to open this?"

"Yes."

She paused, then slowly tugged at the ribbon. "What was your name?" The tissue paper fell on her bare feet, and before I could answer she let out a loud, angry sigh. She looked sharply at me. "Where did you get this?" Then again, her teeth clenched tight over the wad of gum. *"Where did you get this?"*

Everything was getting muddled up. I took a step back and stumbled over a tennis shoe. I tried to explain about Rory and me doing the trailers, and how her mother had died and her brother had sold us the trailer and I had done the cleaning. But I could tell it wasn't making any sense because she just kept staring at me, forehead all tense, eyes a dull hard blue, nothing at all like they were in the picture.

"Let me guess, you're from her church." She shook her head. "You people are unbelievable. First the phone calls and now this little visit."

"No . . . I just want to give you the picture. I'm . . . a friend." My voice sounded desperate and wavery but I couldn't make it stop.

She scoffed. She looked down at the picture again, her face different now, almost peaceful except for something ugly and hard around her eyes. "Look at that necklace. I was so proud of that thing." She shook her head real slow. But then something was building again, and her jaw moved forward until the sharp tips of her bottom teeth showed beneath her top lip. Her narrowed eyes looked at me but her words were spoken to everything around us: the heavy air, the house with its peeling paint, the overgrown weeds pushing against the steps. "I wasn't the daughter she hoped for and she never let me forget it. I'm sure as hell not going to let you people rub my nose in it now that she's dead." She stared at something far behind me.

Finally she looked at me again, eyes clear, and held the picture back out to me. "Hang it up in the church if you want. Goodbye."

I took it. Took my Tabby. I looked again at the picture, and eyes and hair and sweater and halter top and ponytail were all swimming in front of me, all mixed up and in the wrong places. I felt confused and sick and wondered why everything was toppling away from me: the house, the doorway, the woman standing there, the railing beside me. My eyes blurred with tears and I waved my hand toward her like some crazy person. "It's for you," I said. "Please."

"Jesus Christ!" she groaned, then spun around and went back into the house, slamming the door. A few seconds later I could hear the TV turned up loud.

I stood there, staring at the door. Finally I put the picture down on the cracked cement. An ant appeared from under a shoe and scurried toward the picture, climbing the frame and running all willy-nilly across Tabby's sweater and then along her chin. I backed down the steps and stumbled again at the bottom. The weeds pulled at my nylons but I didn't care about the snags.

I got into the car and drove quickly, staring straight ahead. I was almost at the Miami River bridge when I noticed the box with the butterfly still sitting on the passenger seat. I parked on the shoulder and walked out to the middle of the bridge. I stood at the railing and watched the water flow under the bridge, dark and warm and green. I remembered Diane leaping downwards, a flash of tanned skin, flying, and then in one terrible splash, gone. I'd hold my breath, waiting, watching, knowing she was somewhere under those tons of water. And then I'd see her slick head, laughing, smiling, waving. Swimming over to the edge of the river, climbing the cement steps that gouged the steep bank and led back to the road. Back to me.

I held the butterfly in my palm. I slowly spread my fingers until it slipped off. It sparkled as it fell, twisting this way and that. Then it was on the water, bobbing gently, being pulled forward by the current. It moved faster and faster, and even before it floated past the cement steps I knew it was gone for good.

BIRD WATCHING

by Kate Seegraves

Julie lay on her stomach across Margot's bedroom floor. She propped up her chin in one hand and absently picked at the rug with the other. Margot sat on the bed, tossing a tennis ball at the ceiling. Its yellow fuzz lightly brushed the plaster before returning to her palms with a soft *thud*. The open window ushered in the sounds of Xenia in June: lawnmowers, birds, and the occasional passing airplane.

Two weeks out of school, and they were already bored.

Julie sighed and rolled onto her back, counting the roses in the wallpaper.

"This," Margot said, "is lame."

Julie nodded. She raised her head to look at her friend. "Got any ideas?"

Margot shrugged. The gum in her mouth popped. "We could go to the pool."

Julie rolled her eyes. She knew Margot had no interest in actually swimming. The lifeguard, Matt Perkins, was a hot senior at Xenia High School. He played quarterback for the football team and worked at the community pool in the summer. Margot said he looked like a tan Robert Pattinson. At Margot's insistence, they spent their entire vacation last year strutting around the pool deck in new bikinis, hoping to catch his eye. The only thing either of them caught was vicious sunburn. Julie doubted Matt Perkins noticed eighth graders much, unless they were drowning, yet she had let Margot talk her into returning, day after day. Not that Julie had protested much. This summer, however, she had hoped for a different routine.

"Nah," Julie said. "It's not sunny enough." She ran her tongue across her braces, a habit she had developed during middle school. "What about the mall? Mom could drive us." Julie pictured her mother next door, hanging laundry to dry on the backyard clothes line.

Margot made a face. "The mall is boring. And I'm too fat to go shopping."

"Are not."

"Am, too."

"Whatever."

The girls lapsed into silence again. Outside, a dog barked in the distance. Julie thought she could hear her mother's wet laundry flapping in the breeze.

"Maybe we could—"

Margot dropped the tennis ball. It rolled softly off the bed and bounced across the rug. She looked at Julie from her perch and grinned.

"We could bird watch," she said. Her eyes glittered.

Julie stared back at her, unimpressed. "Bird watching?" she asked. "Isn't that for old people?"

Margot shook her head, swinging her feet to the floor. "Not this kind of bird watching," she said. "Hang on." She padded across the room and out the bedroom door, her long hair swinging behind her. She returned several moments later with a heavy black pair of binoculars. Julie guessed Margot swiped them from her dad, an avid hunter.

Margot closed the door and locked it with a flourish. "So my mom doesn't bug us," she said, wiggling her eyebrows. "Come on, I gotta show you this."

Margot crossed the rug and sat next to the window, placing the binoculars on the windowsill. She patted the floor next to her impatiently. Julie sighed and sat up, scooting on her rear end until she and Margot were shoulder to shoulder.

Margot raised the binoculars and pointed them out the window.

She gazed silently for a moment, reaching up occasionally to adjust the main focus.

Julie sighed again. "I don't see why some stupid birds are such a big deal."

"You'll see. Hang on a second." Margot gave the binoculars a final tweak and passed them to Julie. "There. Take a look at that."

Julie obediently raised the binoculars and scanned the horizon. Margot's house sat on top of a modest hill, and her bedroom occupied the home's attic floor. From this vantage point, Julie could see the Xenia's tiny downtown, at the heart of which sat the courthouse and the Greene County Jail. The courthouse clock tower read 12:32. Julie's stomach grumbled. She realized she had not yet eaten lunch, and considered returning home for a sandwich. Instead, she remained at the window, shaking her head slightly.

"What am I looking for, exactly?" she asked.

"You'll know," Margot said, nudging her in the ribs with an elbow. Julie was about to ask what that meant when movement caught her eye. She swung the binoculars north until they landed on the jail.

Julie had noticed the jail's rooftop basketball court many times, of course. The chain-link cage on top of the otherwise bland building was hard to miss. She had never seen the court occupied, however. Now a game was in full swing, five on five, with three thick-necked bailiffs watching courtside. Men, some with sculpted arms and blurred tattoos, others with pale, flabby bodies, charged back and forth in the heat. The court cooked under the sun, making their feet and legs shimmer, mirage-like. Many of the players had pulled off their orange prison shirts, which lay in small fluorescent heaps next to the bailiffs. Sweat stained their white undershirts, and in some cases, trickled down their bare chests.

"Cool, huh?" Margot said suddenly, making Julie jump. She realized with embarrassment that her mouth was hanging open. Blushing, she passed the binoculars back to Margot, who laughed.

"How long have you been watching them?" Julie asked.

"Not long. A few days." Margot looked pleased with herself. "I found them by accident. I actually wanted to know if I could see Matt Perkins' house from here. He lives down the hill on Redburn." Margot turned her gaze to the window again. "It feels like a movie, doesn't it? Like something we'd see on TV or something. I already have my favorites picked out."

"Favorites?"

"Yeah, like, favorite guys. A few of them are hot. I've made up names for them." She turned to Julie. "I call it bird watching because they're jailbirds. Get it?"

Julie nodded. Lunch was all but forgotten. Margot had a crazy imagination, but this was . . . well, interesting.

"Gimme the binoculars," she said. "I want to look again."

Margot passed them back.

"I'll tell you who I've named so far," she said.

***

The girls wrote the fictional names and histories of the men in a spiral notebook with Taylor Lautner on the cover. Their mutual favorite Margot had already dubbed "Caleb McCray," a name they agreed was subtly sexy. He was a regular in the lunchtime games and looked to be the youngest of the players, possibly nineteen or twenty years old. He had deep dimples and long, black hair he wore in a ponytail. Margot said she didn't think a boy with dimples like that could be a hard criminal. They decided he was serving time for cigarette thefts from the Route 68 service station. During the evenings, he wrote poetry in his cell and dreamed of becoming a carpenter.

Caleb hung out with a tall big-nosed man on team they named "Skinny Pete." He had the look of a drug dealer, Julie said. They imagined he was serving a year for selling and distributing pot. He was no match physically for some of the other basketball players, outweighed by at least forty pounds, but the men let him play because he was funny and had a mean streak.

The fat man they most often saw puffing through the games they called "Tom the Tulip," so named for the flower tattoo on his right bicep. Tom, they determined, was a florist in his life outside.

"What's Tom in for?" Julie asked, three days after she and Margot began watching the games in earnest. She sat with her legs crossed on the floor, the open notebook in her lap. At the window, Margot lowered the binoculars and drummed her fingers on her knee.

"Burglary?" she suggested. Julie shook her head.

"He's too fat."

"How about money laundering?"

"Perfect." Julie bent over the notebook, pen scribbling. "He's a white collar criminal. He sends his mother red tulips every year on her birthday."

"Yeah, that's good." Margot sighed a little wistfully. "Isn't Caleb hot?"

"Yeah," Julie agreed. It was true. He was good looking, no doubt. It was the dimples, she thought. Neither of them mentioned Matt Perkins the entire afternoon.

***

The days grew hotter. For once, Margot didn't complain about the house's lack of air conditioning. It was easier to see the basketball court if the window was open, she said, and the heat made the inmates take off their shirts.

Three weeks passed. Julie spent every afternoon in Margot's bedroom, watching. The notebook's stories grew more detailed. Caleb's poetry was about an ex-girlfriend who broke his heart. Skinny Pete ran an illicit contraband ring inside the jail–his sister brought him banned goods hidden in containers of oatmeal cookies. Tom the Tulip owed Skinny Pete fifty cigarettes for a deck of playing cards.

"Who do you think would win in a fight, Caleb or Matt Perkins?" Julie asked Margot one July afternoon. The basketball game had ended for the day—the girls lounged side by side on the rug, snacking on Oreos straight from the package.

Margot thought for a moment, chewing on a cookie. "Caleb," she said. "Matt's strong, but Caleb's probably seen lots of prison fights. I bet he's learned some stuff on the inside."

They didn't speak after that. They stared at the spinning ceiling fan, lost in daydreams.

***

The following afternoon, twenty minutes into the basketball game, Tom the Tulip pushed Caleb. It came suddenly and without warning—Caleb had positioned himself for a shot near the three-point line when Tom planted his meaty palms between the younger man's shoulder blades, shoving him to the hot cement. Julie, who had the binoculars, gasped.

"What? What's wrong?" Margot grabbed for the binoculars, but Julie swatted her away.

"Tom just pushed Caleb." Julie watched intently. Caleb regained his feet and rubbed his elbows with a grimace. His mouth worked angrily around curses Julie could only guess at. Tom stood nearby, laughing.

"What's happening?" Margot asked.

"Caleb's up now. He looks pissed." She passed Margot the binoculars.

"Oooh," Margot said. "Drama. Write it down. A jailhouse feud or something."

"Got it." Julie flipped to a new page and clicked the pen. "They must hate each other."

"Yeah," Margot agreed. "That's intense."

***

The next day, Julie arrived later than usual at Margot's. She came in through the back door and stomped up the stairs to the attic, her flip flops smacking against her heels.

"Hey, sorry I'm late," she called as she ascended. "Mom made me vacuum the living room before I could—"

The bedroom door flew open. Margot stood on the other side with wide eyes.

"Get in here," she hissed. "Something's happening."

"What? Another fight?" Julie hurried into the room as Margot shut and locked the door. The girls sank to their knees at the window.

"I dunno," Margot said. "But something's wrong. Here, look." She passed the binoculars.

Julie scanned the court. The game moved along as usual, but Caleb had taken a break from the action. He stood on the sideline instead with a water bottle raised to his lips, watching the remaining players rush from basket to basket. His face was curiously blank, and it made Julie nervous.

"You're right," she said. She felt tightness in her chest. She could hear Margot's breath quickening. "Caleb looks weird."

Skinny Pete suddenly signaled for a time out. He approached Caleb's side of the court and also reached for a water bottle. The other men lingered near center court, aimlessly passing the ball. Tom the Tulip stood at the foul line on the far end of the court, practicing his free throw. As Skinny Pete sipped his water, Julie saw him pass something to Caleb, who quickly palmed the object from his left hand to his right. It was white and pointy. It looked like a plastic spoon with sharpened edges, she thought.

With dawning comprehension, Julie realized it was more than a spoon. Her stomach dropped.

Pete and Caleb tossed their water bottles aside, and the game resumed. Tom the Tulip snagged a rebound and began moving the ball to the opposite basket. Caleb guarded him closely. Suddenly, Tom drove toward the basket, angling for a clumsy layup. Instead of blocking him, Caleb sprang forward. His dimples drew back in a grimace as he drove the homemade knife into the soft folds of Tom's neck. Tom's mouth formed a grotesque "O" of surprise as the wound began spraying blood.

Julie screamed.

Tom crumpled to the ground. Sweat and bright red droplets mingled on his round cheeks.

Margot ripped the binoculars from Julie's hands and pointed them at the court. Her face turned white. "Oh my God!" she shrieked. Julie could not reply. She smashed her fists against her mouth to stifle another scream. Her braces bit into her lips.

"What do we do?" Margot's breath came in short bursts. "They're . . . They're taking Caleb. Oh my god, they're cuffing him. There's so much blood. Oh my God, Julie, what do we do??" Margot dropped the binoculars to the rug and turned to Julie. "We have to call somebody. We have to call the police!"

Julie spoke through her fingers. "Margot, it's the jail. Those are the police." She could feel her head getting light and urged herself not to faint.

"But we have to do something!" Margot's voice rose in pitch until it became a loud, desperate whine. "We have to do something! We can't just let him die!"

A firm knock at the door made them jump. "Girls, what's going on?" Margot's mother, her voice muffled but stern, filtered through the door. "Why are you both screaming?"

"It's nothing!" Margot said, and laughed shakily. "No worries, Mom. We're watching a movie."

"All right," her mother said after a slight pause. "Try to keep it down, okay?"

"Okay!" the girls said in unison. They listened as Margot's mother retreated, her footsteps creaking down the hall.

Margot and Julie stared at the binoculars on the floor. The room felt heavy with heat.

"What do we do?" Margot repeated softly. Her eyes remained downcast. Julie shifted her gaze to Margot's pale, scared face. She was suddenly overcome with a violent urge to hit her, to claw at her face and scratch at her eyes. This had been her idea. This was Margot's fault.

Instead, Julie stood and walked slowly to the bedroom door. She unlocked it and laid her hand on the knob.

"I don't think I'm coming over tomorrow," she said, and let herself out.

***

Julie stayed in bed the next day. She ignored Margot's repeated efforts to contact her—texts, mostly, although she thought she heard Margot knock on the front door once. That night, Julie's mom brought her dinner on a TV tray. First she asked if Julie felt sick. Then she asked if she'd had a fight with Margot.

"No," Julie said. "We're just . . . I just don't think I want to hang out with her anymore." Her mother didn't press, and Julie didn't offer an explanation. She wasn't sure she could explain it anyway. She ate her dinner listlessly, moved the tray to the floor and fell into a troubled sleep.

Two weeks went by before she saw Margot again. It was a Saturday morning. Julie and her mother were going shopping for back-to-school clothes. Julie exited the house first, climbing into the family minivan parked in the driveway. As Julie's mom hopped into the driver's seat and started the engine, Margot came onto her front porch. She took a few uncertain steps toward them and stopped. Julie's mom backed the van into the street.

Julie studied her friend through the windshield. Her face looked pinched and tired.

"You want to talk to her?" her mom asked.

Julie shook her head. "No. Let's go."

Julie's mom shifted into drive and pulled away from the house. Julie watched Margot in the side mirror until they turned a corner. Margot and her house vanished from view.

Julie leaned back into the seat. She felt older than fourteen. She reached forward and clicked on the radio, catching the end of a rock song by a band she didn't recognize. Julie found herself wondering how dark Matt Perkins' tan was by now. She decided she didn't really care.

MOTIVE

by LD Masterson

Marv Carczek hated working homicides in the park. Especially Washington Park. For one thing, it was only a couple blocks from District One's house, which was kind of insulting to the department. More than that, he liked this park. It was his little oasis in the heart of downtown Cincinnati. He liked the sounds of birds and kids and people enjoying themselves. But this morning there was an unnatural stillness. The birds had taken their music elsewhere, and the small cluster of joggers and bystanders gathered outside the yellow tape spoke in hushed tones. As if murder in such a beautiful spot deserved more respect than murder on the back streets of Over-the-Rhine.

Marv had reached the crime scene first. He wanted to be there when his new partner arrived. He hated breaking in a new partner. He and Mueller had worked well together. Solid. Until Mueller's arthritic knees forced him into early retirement. Marv had met Sara Ryan for the first time yesterday, Ryan and her brand new gold shield. How'd he get stuck with a wide-eyed kid who looked barely old enough to drive? And when had they started giving detective shields to children?

Couldn't refuse to take her on though. Not once the lieutenant had made the pairing. He'd have to deal with her for a month or so and then he could say it wasn't a good fit and asked for a reassignment. Unless she helped him out by screwing up big time before then.

She was only minutes behind him and he watched her approach. Dressed right for the job, at least. Slacks, light jacket over a high collared shirt, flat boots. She wore her dark hair in a short no nonsense cut but it didn't overcome the "cute." A uniform lifted the yellow tape to let her pass. Didn't have to lift it far. So damned little. How could he count on her to have his back when he'd have to be constantly watching hers?

"Detective Carczek," she greeted him.

Marv gave her a short nod. "Ryan."

"What have we got?"

Marv tipped his head toward the body. "You tell me."

Ryan met his look squarely then nodded.

Yeah, she got the message. He was putting her through her paces, seeing how she worked the scene. Good. If it made her nervous, he'd get to see how she handled that, too.

She stepped forward, carefully scanning the area. The body lay just off the path but was screened by a line of tall flowering shrubs. Ryan walked slowly around the body as she began her narrative, pausing and stooping to get a closer look when needed.

"Our victim is female, Caucasian, mid-thirties with brown hair. About five-four, one-thirty. Apparent stab wound to the chest. There's a laceration on her left hand, possible defensive wound. No other signs of a struggle. No sign of sexual assault."

Yeah, he had checked for that, and felt the familiar twinge of relief. Even after thirty-five years on the job—most of them with homicide—rape-murders still raked at his gut.

"I'd say from the blood spatter and pooling, she was killed here." Ryan paused and squatted on her heels. "The victim's jewelry is missing. There are visible tan lines for several rings and a watch. That abrasion on her neck could have come from a necklace being torn off, but there's no tearing on her ears. If she was wearing earrings, which seems likely, they were removed more carefully." She looked up at Marv. "Any sign of a purse or a bag?"

"No. Nothing yet." Okay, so far the kid was doing pretty good. He'd grant her that. Hadn't missed anything she should have seen.

Ryan straightened and took a slow look around them. "She wasn't just out for a stroll in the park. Wrong shoes, wrong wardrobe. She was cutting through on her way somewhere else. Or on her way home. From work, shopping, maybe meeting someone . . . she would have had a purse, possibly a bag or a briefcase. Who found her?"

"Jogger. Jogger's dog," he amended.

"These bushes would have given some coverage but he'd have to work fast. Grab and drag or lure her off the path. My first take would be a robbery gone wrong. Or something meant to look like a robbery gone wrong."

"You know about this string of robberies?" Over a dozen in the past few weeks. All women, alone, by a guy with a knife.

"Uh huh," she stopped and looked at Marv. "But none were here in the park, and none of the victims were injured."

He knew that. He wasn't saying it was the same guy, but somehow her dismissal made him want to push the possibility. "Not until now. You just said yourself, a robbery gone wrong." He gestured toward the body. "That would be the 'gone wrong'."

For a moment he thought she was going to argue with him then she simply nodded and turned her attention back to the body.

***

Their victim's name was Laura Knott. Missing Persons, even when it was too early to open a case, routinely forwarded information to the morgue. Laura's description had been called in by her husband Gerald when she failed to come home the night before. They found Gerald at home and Marv delivered the standard notification of next of kin. It was not his favorite part of the job.

"I'm sorry for your loss," Marv told him.

"Dead? But . . . when? How? An accident?" Knott looked back and forth between Marv and Ryan in disbelief.

"I'm sorry, Mr. Knott, but your wife was murdered." Marv steered him to a chair and eased him into it then sat opposite him. Knott was tall and fit with an expensive haircut and a fresh manicure, but the shadowed eyes and tight expression spoke of a sleepless and anxious night.

"Murdered? How? Where?"

Marv let the first question slide, answered the second. "Washington Park."

"The park. Yes, she always walked through the park on her way home. Even at night. She said it was quicker and she liked the flowers, you see, and . . ." His words trailed into silence.

Marv glanced at Ryan, who stood slightly behind him and off to the side, pen and notebook in hand. Right where she was supposed to be, he ceded, close enough to see Knott's reactions but far enough away to be ignored.

"Do you know where was she coming from, Mr. Knott?" Marv asked.

"Last night? Work. Jackie Deer Catering. She had to work late . . . they've got this big thing coming up at Findlay Market. We both worked late. I had a backlog of paperwork and since I knew she wouldn't be home for dinner, I stayed at the office to get it done. I got home a little after midnight. But she wasn't here. She never works later than nine. I called her cell, her office, even a couple friends—girls she works with, but I knew if she'd been with a friend she would have called me. She'd never be that late without calling me. That's when I called the police. But they said it was too soon. I had to wait twenty-four hours. Twenty-four hours. And now you tell me she's dead."

"Sir, you said you were working late. Where do you work?"

"I'm an accountant. With Dwire and Franc." Knott answered absently, as though he was still trying to come to terms with the news they had brought him.

"And where is your office?"

"Mercantile Center. On Walnut."

Marv nodded. He knew the building. "Was there anyone else in the office last night?"

"No. I don't think so. Why does that . . . wait a minute! What are you saying? That I killed my wife? That I killed Laura. I loved my wife!" Now there was anger, outrage. It was a common reaction, of both the innocent and the guilty.

"We have to ask," Marv told him calmly.

"Yeah, like you had to wait twenty-four hours before you went looking for her. You might have saved her."

"No. Your wife was killed between nine and eleven last night. Well before you came home."

All the anger seemed to desert Knott, and he slumped back in the chair and rubbed his hands over his face.

"Mr. Knott, do you know of anyone who would have wanted to harm your wife?"

"No," Knott shook his head slowly. "Not Laura. Everyone loved her."

Not everyone. "Did she have any close friends we could talk to?"

"Um, the girls she worked with. It's a small company and they're pretty tight." Knott seemed to stir himself. "Where is she? Where's Laura? I need to see her."

Marv took out a card and laid it on the low table between them. "When you're ready, call this number. They'll tell you where to go."

Ryan followed Marv out of the apartment, but neither spoke until they reached the street.

"What do you think?" he asked her.

"He's lying," she answered easily. "About where he was last night, at least. He gave off pretty much every tell in the book. Way too much detail. Sounded rehearsed to me."

Marv gave her a sidelong glance. So she'd caught that, too. "Yeah. He wasn't working late. I'm smelling girlfriend. Which could be motive. Or just bad timing. We'll have to see."

The next several hours gave them nothing in the way of leads. A visit to Deer Catering confirmed Laura Knott and four others had worked until nine the night before. As her husband said, Laura had been tight with her coworkers and the interviews were full of disbelief and tear-swollen eyes. No one could offer any possible reason for someone to have killed her.

Their canvass of the park had done no better. The beautiful spring day was no match for the harsh reality of yellow police tape and many of the park's regulars had stayed away. Marv and Ryan found a few people who recognized Laura's photograph but no one who had seen her last night. Not surprisingly, they'd also come up empty on her knife-wielding assailant.

They returned to their car and Marv eased into the heavy downtown traffic. His new partner had not been foolish enough to suggest she drive.

"I'm hungry," Marv said abruptly. He motioned toward the local chili place down the block. "Let's grab some lunch before we head back to the House." A quick glance. "Or don't you eat? You one of those women who starve themselves so they can wear a size whatever?"

Ryan's cheeky grin made her look even younger. Twelve, maybe thirteen.

"No, I'm one of those women who eat like a horse and hope I can stay active enough to burn it off."

They stuck to small talk over lunch. Sports mostly. Ryan agreed with him that the latest Reds acquisition was a waste of money. Good baseball talk mellowed Marv to the point that he asked a question he'd planned not to ask.

"So, Ryan, why a cop?"

The stiffness in her smile told him she'd answered this question too many times. "I just thought I had the right look. Tailor made for the uniform, don't you think?"

He reached for a response and came up empty. The silence drew out just a beat too long before she let him off the hook.

"Actually, it's genetic. Runs in the family."

"Your father was on the job?"

He saw a hint of disappointment in her eyes and something else, something that made him feel slightly ashamed.

"No, my mother."

***

There were two reports waiting on his desk when they returned. Marv kept the autopsy and tossed the lab report onto Ryan's desk, across from his, front edges touching. "Not much here," he commented as he read. "Single thrust. Nothing distinctive about the blade. Slight angle suggests the killer was right-handed. Victim last ate about seven hours before her death, so she didn't stop for dinner. No alcohol in her system, no drugs. Overall good health . . . except for being stabbed."

"Lab came up empty, too." Ryan scanned the other report. "No fibers, hair, or blood that wasn't the victim's. Nothing under her nails. Her pockets were empty except for a couple receipts, a grocery list, and a half-dozen old lottery tickets. No usable prints."

Marv turned to his computer. "Got the preliminary financials on Laura; no significant life insurance, no potential inheritance, nothing that would make her death especially profitable to anyone." He gave Ryan a quick look. "I've asked for file copies on those robberies."

She nodded. "What about the husband, lying about where he was last night?"

Marv checked his watch. Yeah, it was time for a follow up. "Okay, let's pay Mr. Knott another visit."

***

It was easy. Too easy. Marv had barely started to push when Gerald Knott folded.

"All right. I wasn't working last night. I . . . I was with a woman. I didn't want to say anything because I knew how it would look. And because . . . I was ashamed. I mean, how do you think I feel? Knowing my wife was killed while I was . . ."

"We're going to need a name," Marv told him.

"I know." Knott pushed one hand through his hair. "But could you do this, um, quietly?" He turned his face slightly away from Ryan and leaned toward Marv. Man to man. "The lady is also married. In fact, she's the wife of a client. If it comes out that we've been . . . seeing each other, it will destroy her marriage." He hesitated then added with a shrug, "And I'll lose my job."

***

"I don't know," Marv told Ryan as they drove through the country style roads of upscale Indian Hill, "all this money, and these people don't even have sidewalks or streetlights. Makes no sense to me."

Ryan snorted lightly but made no comment as they turned into the long circular drive of Randolph and Lia Dunworthy.

Lia Dunworthy was a striking blond, slightly older than Laura Knott, who invited them into her expensive home as though they were welcomed guests. Dunworthy sat on a pristine white sofa while Marv perched on the edge of a matching chair. Ryan took her place, standing just to the side.

"Mrs. Dunworthy, you know why we're here?" Marv asked her.

"Yes, Jerry called me. It's all right. Randolph is at a meeting and it's Marie's day off. We can speak freely." She blushed slightly and looked toward Ryan as if hoping she, rather than Marv, would be asking the questions. He would use that, if he needed to, but not yet.

"Can you tell me where you were last night between the hours of seven and midnight?"

"Yes, of course." Dunworthy's hand played nervously with the multiple strands of gold around her neck. "Oh dear, this is rather awkward, isn't it? I was at The Westin. With Jerry. Gerald Knott."

"What's the nature of your relationship with Mr. Knott?"

"Oh well, that's rather obvious, isn't it? He's my lover. Has been for . . . oh . . . almost six months now."

"Is Mr. Dunworthy aware of your affair?"

"Dolphy?" There was a hint of laughter, as though the question was too absurd to be taken seriously. "Heavens, no."

"To your knowledge, was Mrs. Knott aware of the affair?"

More serious now. "No, I'm quite certain she was not. Jerry and I are always very discreet."

Marv let the silence draw out between them but Dunworthy didn't seem compelled to add any convincing arguments. A sign that she was telling the truth.

"Okay, we need to confirm that you and Mr. Knott were together the whole time, from seven until midnight. Did you go anywhere together, where you might have been separated?"

"Oh, no. We never go out in public together. We met in the room, as we always do. I arrived first and Jerry joined me about ten minutes later."

"And you were together, in the room, the entire time. He didn't step out at all, even for a few minutes." The Westin was maybe eight or nine blocks from Washington Park. A five minute cab ride or easily made on foot.

Dunworthy stiffened, pushing past embarrassment to irritation. "Yes. We were in that room together from just after seven o'clock until after midnight."

"Okay, I have to ask." He offered an apologetic smile to sooth her ruffled feathers. She could be lying but he didn't think so. Still, he might as well keep going, see if he could rule out the most obvious motive.

"Mrs. Dunworthy, did you and Mr. Knott ever discuss changing the nature of your relationship? Possibly leaving your marriages so the two of you could be together?"

"Well, we've talked about it. You know, as people do under the circumstances. I believe Jerry would like something more . . . between us, but he knows I'd never leave Randolph. You see, I like fine things," she glanced around the room inviting Marv's eyes to follow, "expensive things. In fact, I fear I'm shockingly expensive. And Jerry, well, Jerry just couldn't afford me."

Marv closed his notebook and was returning it to his pocket when Ryan slid past him and sat down next to Dunworthy. He tried to frown her away but she missed his signal, or ignored it.

"Mrs. Dunworthy, if I may, just one more question."

Ryan offered a hopeful smile, combined with eyes opened wide.

"Of course, my dear," Dunworthy turned from Marv and all but patted Ryan's hand. "What is it?"

Hell, next Dunworthy will be offering Ryan some milk and cookies.

"You said Mr. Knott didn't go out at all. I was thinking, he probably would have offered you something . . . wine perhaps, or—"

Dunworthy beamed. "Champagne. Yes, Jerry is so thoughtful. He ordered champagne. From room service."

"Oh, I love champagne. I can't drink too much though," Ryan said with a sheepish smile. "The bubbles always go right to my head."

"I know." Dunworthy gave an almost girlish giggle. "It makes me quite tipsy."

"And then I get sleepy."

"Well, you know that's odd because it doesn't usually do that to me, but now that you mention it, I did feel very drowsy last night."

"Did you fall asleep?"

Dunworthy frowned with the effort of remembering. "I'm not sure. I might have. I think I did, for a few minutes." The frown lines faded. "In fact, Jerry did, too. I remember because I woke up and he was still asleep with his head on my—" A quick glance at Marv. "Well, he was sound asleep. So he couldn't have left the room if that's what you were thinking."

Marv waited until they had taken their leave of the Dunworthy mansion and were headed back downtown before jumping on Ryan.

"You want to let me know the next time you intend to break into an interview like that?"

Ryan stiffened but kept her voice level. "It looked to me like you were finished. And I had a couple questions of my own."

"Yeah, like did they doze off after sex. And they did. And you think that pokes a big hole in Knott's alibi."

"Doesn't it?"

Of course it did. And Marv knew he had dropped the ball by not asking the question himself. That rankled. "Yeah, maybe. But you still need motive."

"Knott was cheating on his wife."

"Oh hell, Ryan, that doesn't mean anything. If every guy who ever cheated on his wife was a murderer we'd have to arrest half the men in this city. Including me."

Damn. Where did that come from? Ancient history. No bearing here. Why had he even thought about it?

He knew why.

"All right. You're so hung up on the husband for this, tomorrow you do some digging. You come up with some kind of solid motive to go with the questionable alibi and I'll take another look at him. In the meantime, I'm going to work those robbery files."

***

They spend the morning on their separate tasks, Marv searching for a possible connection between their case and the recent string of robberies, Ryan pouring through Knott's finances, phone records, and personal history. By noon, Marv was fairly convinced he was following the wrong trail. He hoped Ryan was having better luck. And he didn't. It gnawed at him. No matter what he felt about having this little girl foisted on him for a partner, the job had to come first. Catch the bad guy *then* worry about Sara Ryan.

Finally Ryan stretched, arching her back, and ran her hands over her face as if to wipe away fatigue.

"I'm getting nothing," she told him. "No hidden money, no family connections on Laura's side that Knott would need to hang on to, no unusual risk of scandal. If Gerald Knott wanted to dump his wife, it would have been easy enough to divorce her. No need to kill her."

He was more disappointed than relieved and was vaguely pleased by that.

"Okay, how about this?" he offered. "Dunworthy wasn't just Knott's alibi, he was hers too."

"What? You like Lia Dunworthy for this?"

"Why not? It wouldn't have been that hard to pull off. Get Gerald to talk about his wife's habits, how she went to and from work, when she'd be coming home that night. Knott goes to sleep, Dunworthy slips out, waits in the park, maybe asks Laura to help her with something, whatever, to get her to stop for a minute, step off the path. Doesn't take much strength to stick a knife in someone, especially if they don't know it's coming. Means and opportunity."

"What about motive? It wasn't as though Laura was standing between Dunworthy and Knott. Lia wasn't going to leave Daddy Warbucks for a lowly accountant."

"Maybe Laura had found out about the affair. Threatened to tell the husband. Lia Dunworthy kills Laura, lets Knott take the fall, and gets to keep her husband and all that nice money."

"That could work both ways. If Laura threatened to tell Randolph Dunworthy, Knott could lose his lover *and* his job." Ryan paused as though turning something over in her mind. "But Laura didn't know about the affair."

"How do you know that?"

"The women she worked with. They *were* close, and they all described her as very happily married. Remember how a couple of them said they were worried about Gerald, how he and Laura were so in love? If she had found out about the affair, someone there would have picked up on it." Ryan shook her head. "No, Laura Knott didn't know about Lia Dunworthy. Which means Lia Dunworthy had no motive."

"Then neither did Gerald Knott."

The stubborn thrust of her chin might have amused him, at some other time, but there was nothing amusing about the cold glint in her eyes. Damn, she just wouldn't let it go.

Marv blew out his breath in a long sigh. "Okay, you like the husband?"

Ryan nodded slowly. "It was the husband."

"What makes you so sure?"

"He knew she was dead. When we went to notify him, he already knew."

"And how do you know that?"

"It was in his eyes."

Now Marv leaned forward and fixed her with a hard stare. "You know, Ryan, you're a little new at this to be basing a whole case on what you think you saw in some guy's eyes. I have no problem with *women's intuition*, but I'd like to see a little more of a track record on yours before I'm ready to lay my money on it."

Several heads turned their way and Marv realized his voice had risen on the wave of frustration. He pushed back his chair and motioned Ryan to follow. At least she didn't argue that. It took three tries to find an empty interview room. He motioned her in ahead of him and barely had the door closed before she whirled and attacked.

"Okay, Carczek, what is it about me you don't like?" Her voice was low and seething with rage. "You think I can't do the job because I look too young? Because I'm too small? I'm a good cop and I busted my hump to make detective and I won't have you brush aside what I saw, what I know, with some crack about women's intuition."

"That wasn't a crack." The words came out of him unbidden, unplanned. Ryan seemed to realize that and she waited for him to continue.

"I have a lot of respect for women's intuition. The best partner I ever had was a woman. Rose Varsi."

Still Ryan waited. The question was there, unspoken.

"She went down in the line. Convenience store, we just walked in on it." The knot in his throat threatened to cut off his words. "She bled out in my arms."

She put it together; he could see her put it together. He had fallen in love with his partner, cheated on his wife with her. And lost her.

"Did you get the guy?" Ryan asked quietly.

"Yeah. Yeah, I got him."

The silence drew out between them. Marv heard the clock on the wall ticking off the seconds. What could he say? Sara Ryan was nothing like Rose but somehow being partnered with Ryan had brought it all churning up from where he'd kept it buried for almost twenty years.

"Look," Ryan said at last, "I'm up against enough in this job. Every other cop on the force looks down at me, literally. I have to show my badge just to walk into a bar. I get challenged on the street twice as much as other cops because I look like an easy mark. Those are my problems and I can deal with them. But I don't need to deal with yours. I'll ask the lieutenant to reassign me to someone else. As soon as we close this case."

Marv crossed over to the table in the center of the small room and perched one haunch on the edge. "Okay. We like the husband for this and we can argue means and opportunity. But that's not going to be enough to move on him."

Ryan started to pace, slowly, head down. "He had it all laid out. Nothing spontaneous. Set up his alibi, with a little something in Lia Dunworthy's drink to put her to sleep, but gave us that story about being at work first."

Marv grunted agreement. "Alibi looks more solid if we find it on our own."

"And he set the scene, taking her jewelry and her bag so we'd think robbery."

It took her two more passes across the room and back. When she stopped, Marv could almost see the light bulb come on over her head.

"I want to go to the lab."

***

A phone call had Laura Knott's personal effects waiting for them when Marv and Ryan arrived. Her clothes were spread out on the steel table but Ryan gave them only a glance. "There were some papers in her pockets."

The young technician motioned toward a brown envelope. "Not much there. Nothing of value. The husband is coming by later today to pick it all up."

Ryan nodded, pulling on gloves before easing the clothing aside and emptying the envelope's contents onto a clear area. She separated the items, dropping the receipts and shopping list back into the envelope and spreading out the lottery tickets. Marv waited quietly while she examined each one.

"The date on this one, something's been spilled on it. Can you make it out?"

Marv studied the piece of paper then shook his head, "No, but it wouldn't matter. Lottery office would validate it by the bar code on the bottom."

Ryan pulled out her cell phone and quickly keyed in a search. It took less than a minute. She turned to Marv with a fierce grin.

"What?" he asked.

"We've got motive."

***

"In here, please, sir." The attendant ushered Gerald Knott into the small room.

"Thank you," Knott murmured then gave a slight start at the site of Marv sitting behind the small table. "Oh, Detective Carczek. I didn't expect to see you here."

"How are you holding up, Mr. Knott?" Marv asked gently, gesturing to the chair nearest Knott.

"Um, okay, I guess." Knott lowered himself into the wooden chair. "I'm trying to make arrangements, you know, for Laura's service." His words trailed off then in a stronger voice he asked, "Do you have any news? I mean, have you found the guy who did this?"

"Not yet. I'm sorry."

The door opened and Ryan came in carrying a small cardboard box. She placed it on the table in front of Knott. "Your wife's effects, sir."

"Thank you, um . . . ." Knott struggled for a name but Ryan turned away and moved around the table to the chair next to Marv's.

"I know this is difficult," Marv told him, "but we need you to compare the contents of the box to the list on the top. To make sure everything is there and so you can tell us if there's anything there that shouldn't be or anything missing other than the list of jewelry you gave us."

Knott nodded. "I understand." He started to reach for the box then rose, pushing his chair to one side. With a visible swallow, he lifted the lid, blanching slightly as he looked at the white blouse folded neatly on top, the cheerful ruffle stiff and dark with blood. He lifted the clothing, piece by piece, without speaking until he had looked at them all. "No, these are all my wife's things; this is what she was wearing when she left the apartment that morning. I don't see anything missing." He hesitated then reached for the small envelope in the bottom of the box, glancing questioningly at Marv.

"There were a few things in her jacket pockets," Marv explained.

Knott nodded again and pulled out the slips of paper. He looked at the receipts first. "Mocha latte. She loved mocha lattes." Knott placed one hand over his mouth as though fighting back a sob.

"Are you okay, sir?"

"Yes, it's just . . ." He moved on to the lottery tickets, glancing at each one. "Uh, there's something wrong here." He turned the list toward Marv. "It says there were six lottery tickets but there are only five here."

Marv looked at the list and watched as Knott spread the five tickets out on the table. He turned to Ryan who simply nodded and left the room. "She's going to check on it," Marv explained.

"I know it sounds foolish but anything, everything she had with her when she died . . . I just want to have."

"No, I understand."

Knott picked up the last item, the shopping list. He began to read. "Lasagna. She was going to make lasagna. It's my favorite." This time the sob did come.

"If this is too hard, we can let you take what's here and we'll send that other lottery ticket on later."

"No, I'm okay. Really." He began to finger the five tickets. "I'd rather finish this now."

"Your wife liked to play the lottery?"

Knott offered him a sad smile. "Loved it. Bought a ticket every week. I used to tell her it was a waste of money—I mean, considering the odds—but she said it was fun, a little exciting, wondering if this one might just be a winner. She never won, but she still played."

At that moment, Ryan re-entered the room and, with a nod for Marv, handed Knott a small piece of paper. The quick relief on Knott's face faded as he looked at the ticket. "Wait a minute. This isn't my wife's ticket."

Marv leaned forward as though trying to read what Knott held in his hand. "What do you mean?"

"It's the wrong location. Look." He pushed the tickets on the table toward Marv and laid the other beside them. "All these came from the same place. Look at the location numbers. And look at this one. It's different."

"Well, maybe your wife bought this one in a different place. Maybe trying to change her luck."

"No. She always bought her tickets in the same place. Look at the location numbers."

"She did," Ryan told Marv. "I noticed that, too." Then, to Knott, "In fact, we checked that location number and found out it's the coffee shop in the Mercantile Center. Your office building, Mr. Knott. It seems a little odd that your wife would walk over a dozen blocks to your office building to buy her tickets when there are so many places closer to home."

Knott's eyes darted from Ryan to Marv. "Well, sometimes she came down and we'd have lunch together. She must have bought the tickets then. Yes, that's right. I remember now, she mentioned it to me once. She thought buying her tickets in my building would bring her luck."

"Then how is it that no one at that coffee shop recognized your wife's picture?" Ryan asked.

"Well, I wouldn't expect them to. Do you know how many people go in and out of that coffee shop every day? How could you expect them to remember one face?"

"They remembered yours. Cappuccino every morning. Lottery ticket every week."

"You bought tickets, too?" Marv asked him. "I thought you said they were a waste of money."

Knott laughed nervously. "Okay, you got me. I was as bad as Laura. Couldn't resist the possibility of that big win." He glanced again at the ticket in his hand. "Um, but this—"

"How is it," Ryan asked, "that your old tickets were found in your wife's pocket?"

"I . . . I don't . . ." Knott looked to Marv as though he would provide an answer.

And Marv obliged. "Hey, I'll bet she found out you were playing the lottery after you told her not to, and she was going to use those old tickets to give you a bad time about it."

It was a straw, but Knott grabbed for it. "Yeah. I bet that's exactly what happened." He managed a weak chuckle. "That Laura, she was going to—"

"Well, that explains the last ticket," Ryan broke in. "The others were all ones you had bought. That last one must have been hers. That would explain the different location."

"No!" The word seemed to echo in the small room and Knott quickly lowered his voice. "I'm sorry. But this is not her ticket. I mean . . . I don't think this was the ticket that was in her . . ." He stopped and Marv saw the realization hit him.

"Because it was this one?" Ryan laid the missing ticket on the table. "You bought this ticket, Mr. Knott. And you hit that big win. You were finally going to have the money you needed to support your very expensive girlfriend."

Knott stared at the ticket, reaching out one hand then letting it fall.

"But first you had to get rid of your wife, and divorcing her now would cost a lot of money. So you killed her. And you tucked that winning ticket in her pocket, along with some bits of worthless paper, knowing it would all come to you after she was dead."

Knott whirled and caught Ryan with a backhand slap that sent her stumbling against his discarded chair. He pushed past her and headed for the door. Marv came to his feet and started around the table, but Ryan recovered her balance and was right behind Knott. She shoved him into the door then grabbed one arm to swing him around while sweeping his feet from under him, dropping him to the floor. Before Marv had cleared the table, Ryan had Knott cuffed and was pulling him to his feet. She gave Marv a short nod, her eyes bright with satisfaction, blood trickling from the corner of her mouth.

"You don't understand," Knott was pleading. "I had no choice. I love Lia. She's the only thing in the world that matters to me. This was my one chance."

"And how many chances did Laura have?" Ryan asked him. "Gerald Knott, you're under arrest for the murder of your wife."

Marv handed his partner a large white handkerchief, nodding toward her bleeding mouth. She took it without comment and let Marv recite the standard Miranda.

***

Day shift was over by the time they got back to the station. They ran into their lieutenant coming out of the squad as they were going in.

"Carczek, Ryan . . . nice job on that Washington Park murder. I heard you got a confession already."

"Ah, Lieutenant—" Ryan began.

Marv cut her off. "Afraid I can't take the credit for this one, LT. It was the little pit bull here. Once she latches on to something, she doesn't let go."

He felt her begin to bristle and turned to her, his eyes full of apology and unspoken question.

She responded with a slow smile that, as usual, made her look twelve . . . except for the knowing twinkle in her eye. "That's okay, old gray bear," she told him, "I'll let you get the next one."

"You got it," he laughed. "Partner."

KAYFABE

by Bill Bicknell

Every Monday night after the matches, my boyfriend Gus and I would go to Cassano's Pizza on North Main Street just to see who'd be there. If he was in town, Rocco was a given, and he was the one everyone came to see anyway. Six-four, maybe six-five, with heavy tree limb arms set into his barrel torso, Rocco was a sight to behold. He'd walk into Hara Arena, pretend to beat the hell out of Sultan Amin, then go to Cassano's and maybe beat the hell out of somebody for real.

That's if you bothered him—or if you bothered a kid. It took a lot to bother Rocco, but that was him. Bothering a kid was quite a bit easier.

That Monday, he trudged in wearing a coat that nearly doubled his size—and he was already built like a tenement, tall and thick and rough around the edges. He kicked the snow off of his wrestling boots and onto the burgundy tile. From our table in the corner, Gus cleared his throat.

"Oh, God," I muttered, burying my face in my hands. "Don't."

But I knew it was pointless to argue. Gus was going to tick Rocco off, and I had decided a long time ago that I was just going to shut up and let him. The first time he'd done it, I'd shut him up. The next dozen times, I started to think he looked good with that perpetual black eye. So I ducked out to the restroom to let him pile on. Maybe he'd change his mind after Rocco painted his face black and blue for him.

"Ladiiiiiiiiiiiiiiies and gentlemen!" he bellowed in that deep redneck baritone of his. He leaned forward and winked. "*Especially* the gentlemen."

God. I let the door shut behind me.

"Please welcome the undisputed, undefeated, unbelievable, unbeatable, and *highly* untouchable heavyweight champion of the wooooooooooooooooooorld . . . Rocco 'Crapstain' Marshall!"

Crapstain. I turned off the faucet and wiped my hands off on my pants with a huff. It was a new nickname every week, each one less clever than the last. It took him about four months before he had to fall back on working scatological. And of course he got away with it. He knew the manager on duty; they were old drinking buddies back in high school.

I peeked back into the dining room to make sure everything was okay. Sure enough, Rocco was heading to the corner booth, not one patron batting an eye at the tired champion. Our table, meanwhile, was covered with crumpled napkins, tokens of appreciation for our resident announcer. It was the only place in the restaurant where the napkins weren't the greasiest thing at the table.

"You're a jackass," I sighed, easing myself back into the booth and punching Gus in the arm.

"Eh," he answered with a mouthful of pizza. "'f I geh anuhva bahck eye . . ."

Swallow.

". . . I'm callin' the damned cops."

"As opposed to the regular cops?"

"Shut up." He stuffed another slice of deluxe in his cheek like it was a plug of tobacco. What a charmer.

I should mention that Gus was my boyfriend. That "was" is important. We're not together anymore. Like most of the things I did in my twenties, it was a bad idea that ended up getting a whole lot worse.

It didn't take too long for things to quiet down again. That's the way things went in Dayton in the winter. There was a shout, and then it all went quiet again. Normally, Rocco would be up by this point, over to our table, making it clear to Gus exactly which limbs were going to be shoved into which orifices. Call the wrestling fake if you must, but when a 260-pound guy with arms the size of Buicks punches you in the face, it's going to hurt.

But there was none of that this time. I stood up again, and this time, Gus grabbed my wrist. "Where you goin' to?"

"To see how Rocco's doing," I said. "He looks hurt."

Gus nearly spat Pepsi all over the table. "You know that's fake, right? That sultan guy ain't even a real sultan."

"I'm not worried about the wrestling, Gus," I said and pulled my arm away. Gus shrugged—more pizza for him.

Rocco's booth was against a far window that looked out on the neighboring record store. A dim bulb cast a yellow light over the plastic red table, where Rocco's thick, dark hand was sliding a shaker of red pepper flakes across the table. His eyes followed every shift of the pepper inside. Next to him on the table, a little portable radio sputtered play-by-play for what sounded like a basketball game. The Pacers? It was the strangest thing—I'd never heard a station that ran Pacers games in this area.

"What's good, Rocco?" I asked. I knew his real name—Darryl Biggers—but I didn't dare say it. There was a carnie code with these wrestlers. The reality of the show didn't end at the doors of the arena. They called it kayfabe, the world of heroes and villains they'd built their shows around. It wasn't enough to put on a good show; kayfabe meant blurring the lines between reality and fantasy. In those times especially, it was a sacred trust among the wrestlers, and I was smart enough to respect it.

"Making folks rich," he answered. A soft, deep voice, like an underground river. "Snow's good, too. Suppose we'll get a lot of it soon. Kids oughta like that."

"You think so? Weatherman said—"

"Don't you trust them TV guys," he interrupted, still without looking up. "It's gonna be a big one. These bones know. Them TV guys ain't nothin' but an empty suit."

I'd never seen him so determined. I knew he was wrong, of course; I didn't believe a word of it when people would tell me about that kind of psychic mumbo jumbo. But I kept quiet and patted him on the shoulder. "Well, I'm not one to argue," I laughed. "Especially not with a big lug like you."

I lowered my hand to his heavy arm and squeezed, and at last he looked up. The lines under his eyes betrayed what the lights of the ring managed to cover: that Rocco Marshall was, for all of his strength and ferocity in the ring, a man in his fifties who probably shouldn't be doing this wrestling thing anymore. The bones he swore could see the future had no more good years left.

"You think I'd harm a hair on that pretty head of yours?" he said. Louder now. Darryl the tired old man giving way to Rocco the champ.

"I don't think you've got the guts to try," I said, grinning back.

A little boy—probably eight or nine—had squeezed in beside me, a pamphlet in his hand. *Monday Night! Show Biz Wrestling at the Hara Arena!* That, of course, meant my time was up, so Rocco clasped my hand—all the way up to my wrist—in his big mitt and squeezed.

"Stay good, Rocco," I said.

"*Mon cheri*," he said, pronouncing every single word the wrong way.

And I left Rocco alone. Back to Gus. If I was lucky, there'd still be pizza left.

***

That night, Rocco was wrong. It didn't snow at all. The air was cold and dry, and the wind blew in from the west. It was a bitter, hateful wind, the kind that doesn't care about warm clothes or insulated walls. I sent Gus home disappointed and lay alone in my townhouse in Englewood, shivering under a scruffy cotton blanket. I fell asleep on the couch and dreamt that the whole sky was falling on my head before Rocco himself propped it on his shoulders, straining like Atlas beneath the weight of everything that ever was.

***

I did my best to avoid Gus the rest of the week. He drove a plow this time of year, taking jobs for the city and rich folks with big driveways when they came. This year, he wasn't very busy, so I lied and told him that my homework was starting to pile up (It was, but I didn't let that stop me from going out for a beer just about every night.). By the time Thursday rolled around, the phone rang.

"We're not going to your stupid wrestling show on Monday," Gus said before I could even say hello.

"Excuse me?" I said, not even giving him a second of dead air.

"Yeah, I am, even if you're not."

"You don't even have a car," he said. "And none of your college buddies or whoever care about the matches. I'm the one who gets you there, and I say we're not going."

I sucked in a bit of air and swallowed. He was technically right—the only type of right that mattered to Gus. "All right, big shot. I'll bite. Why do you suddenly care so much?"

"Your boyfriend Rocco's all over the Hara sign," he answered. "You told me last week that he was off to New York, some kind of big match at Madison Square Garden."

Again, he was right. Rocco had been talking about it for weeks—the big card in the Northeast. Matches in the New England wrestling territories were big events, and even I knew Rocco stood to gain a big chunk of change with a main event match at Madison Square Garden.

"I can't think of any good reason for him to turn down that gig," Gus continued. I'd done something stupid: I'd given him a chance to keep talking. "Except you."

I damn near fell out of my chair. "What!?"

"Don't play dumb with me," Gus said. Cold. Low. "I know what's goin' on. You and him are doin' a little amateur wrestling of your own."

I wanted to slam the phone down right then and there, but I couldn't let him get away with that. But when I tried to answer, all I could manage were two words. "*God*, Gus."

"So it's true?"

"He's almost old enough to be my grandpa!"

"Oh, so it's one of those replace-your-dad things?" Gus snapped. "Come on, you go to those psychology classes, you read all about that Freud guy! That what it is?"

I swallowed hard. "Screw you, Gus. Don't call me again." And I slammed the phone down hard and threw it across the room.

***

He was right, though: I was shut out. None of my friends cared about the wrestling enough to drive to Hara, and they were my ride to and from school. Mom had moved to Tampa just after I graduated; I don't think she ever cared for this town anyway. And Dad . . . well.

Dad was the one who had taken me to the matches years ago before that heart attack took him away from me. He was short and thick and wore glasses the size of Rocco's arms, and he worked in the factory in Moraine screwing manifolds onto overpriced cars. They called him Professor over at the factory, and the name followed him to the matches at Hara the first time he took me backstage. That was when I met Rocco for the first time, twelve years ago, back when he was in top form.

"You're gonna break somebody's heart someday, kid," he'd said, tousling my red hair. "You keep an eye on her, Professor."

He was right, of course, and he gave me an autographed picture and sent me back out to the arena to watch the matches. At that point, Rocco was one of the most popular wrestlers in the country, and his matches at the bigger arenas—from Detroit to Memphis to Atlanta—drew spectators and reporters from all over. I didn't suspect at the time that he'd still be fighting Sultan Amin when I was into my twenties. I figured he'd vanquish him eventually, send him back to the Syrian Desert where he came from, and then move on to a new set of villains. It never really worked out that way.

I remember when I was thirteen and Dad took me to the Hara matches. Jimmy Thompson up at the school had told me something that I knew couldn't be true, but I had to ask anyway. So as the Highwaymen battled the Bogg Twins for the tag team championships, I looked up at Dad, tugged on his shirt sleeve, and leaned up to his ear.

"It's all fake, isn't it?" I asked.

Dad paused. He pushed his glasses back against his face and held them there for a second, and it's only in hindsight that I know this meant he was deep in thought. Then, he put an arm over my shoulder and motioned across the arena, to the thousands of fans who were on their feet cheering as Bradley Bogg fought off the nefarious double-team tactics of his cowboy opponents.

"Most things have a lot of fake in them," he said. "I think this feels real enough."

And that was that. We never talked about it again. Dad got me my job at Hara and drove me to the arena to intern, to bring out coffee and help with makeup or gear or anything I could. It turned out that Dad had been helping run the books for the promotion for years. Rocco told me years later that he'd never asked for pay—just a chance to hang out backstage with the wrestlers he'd grown up admiring. He was a kid again, and he was glad to take me along.

That was why I had to get to Hara. It wasn't just about seeing the matches; it was a way to make a little extra income. It wasn't much— fifteen dollars a night and a bottle of beer—but anything helps in college.

And Gus was going to stop that? Needless to say, I was through with him.

***

On the morning of the 24th when one of my buddies from calculus dropped me off at my front door, an old maroon Corvair coated with rust waited for me in front of my house, growling for want of a muffler. I could see a thick, tall man hunched in the driver's seat, barely tall enough to fit his massive frame into the vehicle.

"*Mon cheri*," his low voice called as I walked past. That horrible pronunciation. Rocco looked out at me with warm eyes and a smile. "Your coach has arrived."

***

"How'd you even know I lived out here?" I asked, clasping Rocco on the arm as the car ambled down Main Street. Rocco had on his hooded jacket and a pair of sweat pants, but I could tell from the poorly fitting jacket that he had on his wrestling gear underneath it all.

"That's your daddy's house, ain't it?" he answered. "I used to cut your daddy's lawn when you was at Scouts. Your daddy paid me a little extra folding money for it."

I winced. "I thought you made good money—"

"I make everybody *else* good money," he interrupted. Flatly. Slowly. He turned a sideways glance in my direction, and I dared not broach the topic again. "Your daddy was a good man. Ain't nobody happy he's gone."

I leaned back in my seat, pulling my jacket against my body to hold in what little heat the old car could contain. Rocco was right; there was no way I could've found out that my favorite wrestler was mowing my dad's lawn. Kayfabe. Rocco was Rocco.

"Madison Square Garden, though," I said. "That's a big show to turn down."

Rocco nodded. "They'd billed it as a wrestlin' legends match. I was gonna fight 'Bigshot' Billy Holder for the title."

"*Holder?*" I repeated, stunned. A headlining match at Madison Square Garden against the most famous wrestler in the country could've brought home a huge payday—even as someone outside the business, I knew that. And if Rocco was that hard up for money that he took whatever odd jobs he could to pay the bills . . .

"Why?" The only question I could manage.

Sadness fell over the old man's face as he spoke. "Didn't see myself there. Besides, you're gonna need me here. I was wrong about that snow."

"Yeah, but nobody's—"

"It's comin' this week," he continued. "Just a couple days from now. And the kids ain't gonna like it one bit."

I didn't know what to say. The weather had been chilly, but this was Ohio, where summers were humid and winters were bitter. "How do you know that?" I asked.

"I seen it. I seen lots of it; I just didn't know when it was gonna go down. It's almost here. And I'm gonna need your help."

I shook my head. "Rocco—"

"Your boyfriend's got a snow plow, don't he?"

I blinked, jaw agape. I'd never told Rocco that Gus had a plow. I'd only been with Gus for a few months; how did he know that?

"Y-yeah," I stammered.

With a heavy sigh, Rocco gripped the wheel tightly as he turned the car down Shiloh Springs Road—almost to Hara. Once again, he let his eyes brighten, let his smile creep upward, let the champ take over. But there was no questioning that his shoulders seemed to sag under a weight that I didn't yet understand.

"Tonight's gonna be my retirement match," he said. "Don't you tell nobody, but I'm droppin' the title to that young fellow Blakely. I'm only tellin' you this because after today, we got work to do. And I need your help."

Once again—as he'd done so many times in my life—Rocco left me speechless. I wiped a small tear from the corner of my eye. It was no small thing what Rocco had done by telling me what was going to happen. He'd let me in on the fantasy, brought me behind the curtain. Wrestlers were notoriously protective about the business, and even though I'd been an intern for years, this was the first time I'd known the results of the match coming in. I was on the inside of the kayfabe world.

"I'll do what I can," I said.

***

That night, against the backdrop of five thousand screaming fans, the legendary Rocco Marshall lay down in the ring for the last time. In a rare encounter between two heroic babyface wrestlers, the up-and-coming strongman "Bulldozer" Bob Blakely managed to drop the giant champion with his patented German suplex, the arena thundering with the collision of Rocco's heavy shoulders against the mat. The fans cheered their hearts out at seeing the underdog finally get his due as the referee counted the pin. Over the house PA, the emphatic voice of Mr. Pomerville the ring announcer rang forth: "Ladies and gentlemen, your winner, and *new* United States Heavyweight Champion . . . 'Bulldozer' Bob Blakely!"

I clapped from the front row and forced myself to smile. Bob was a nice guy—the son of a factory man like Dad. Just like I'd grown up seeing Rocco lock horns with Sultan Amin, so too would the kids in this arena make Bob their hero. He'd do good by them, I hoped, just like Rocco had done good by me.

As Bob left toward the locker room, wearing Rocco's title belt around his thick waist, all eyes finally turned back to the ring, where the former champion had pulled himself against the corner turnbuckle, wiping his sweaty forehead with a towel. I'd never seen him suck wind like he did after that match, his knees shaking as he grabbed the ring ropes and pulled himself to his feet before collapsing into the top rope, his arms hanging over the top rope like laundry on the line. He looked out, nearly glass-eyed, at the front row, where our eyes met. I gave him a simple thumbs up and mouthed, "You did good, Rocco."

In that moment, his face lit up, and that massive smile crossed his face again. Clutching his side, he dropped to the mat and rolled out of the ring towards me. He reached and pulled me in for a hug, wrapping his thick, sweaty arms around my shoulders, one big hand on the back of my head.

"Almost time," I heard him whisper. "Thursday morning at nine—at the post office on the corner of National and Main. Your boyfriend's gonna be out drinking night before. We need his plow. Bundle up."

And before I could ask the thousands of questions that were pressing heavily on my mind, Rocco was off to the next fan, slapping hands and taking in the warm embrace of the ones who had followed his storied career for so long. If I'd known then what I know now, I'd have understood why he soaked it in like he did.

***

In all honesty, I stewed about it for as long as I could. I stayed home from school on Tuesday and Wednesday, and I'd tell them I had the flu if they asked. It was one thing to leave Gus—one very wonderful thing, I thought—but stealing his plow? Because one of my dad's friends told me to?

But Rocco shouldn't have known that plow was there at all. I was sure of that. Something strange was happening, something that I couldn't hope to explain back then. I was going to steal that plow, and I was going to drive it to National and Main because . . . why?

I didn't know then, but watching the news the night before, it suddenly made sense. I took in the newscaster's words with shock, even as the rain poured outside.

"A storm of unprecedented magnitude will enter the Miami Valley tomorrow morning. Winds are expected to gust up to seventy miles per hour, with snow, freezing rain, and a significant chance for accumulation. The National Weather Service is advising all residents to remain in their homes for the duration of the storm, and please . . ."

I couldn't focus. All I could think about was what Rocco had said. Gus would be out drinking; I was sure of it. With that plow he could make a killing plowing parking lots and driveways for rich people, and his pickup truck—the one his dad had gotten him—was big enough to get him there and back in the snow. He wasn't going to plow streets. There wasn't enough money in that. And if Rocco knew the plow was there . . .

Don't ask me how I rationalized it myself, but as dawn broke the next morning I was outside in gloves, boots, and a parka, stomping through the wet mud to walk the half mile to Gus's house.

***

More than anything else, the wait at National and Main was the worst part. Sitting in the parking lot of that post office, watching the rain turn from water to ice, hearing the wind slowly pick up from a light breeze to cruel gusts, seeing the first few fat snowflakes fall onto the soaking wet snow plow . . .

Getting the keys had been easy. Gus's back door was never locked, the dog didn't bark because he knew me, and the keys to the plow were on the mantle next to his old Smith & Wesson pistol. One bullet in the chamber—that's all he said he'd ever need to put an intruder down. I think it almost killed Gus that he'd never gotten to use it.

It was almost like a dream, feeling the plow roar to life as I backed it out of the driveway, then drove it down the street, across the dam, back to the post office where Rocco had told me to wait. Nearly the moment I put the car into park, the weather turned from warm and wet to a new evil. When I got older, they called it the Great Blizzard, the Blizzard of '78, a whole lot of names. At the time, all I knew was that Rocco was right; it was going to be a big one.

Luckily, he didn't make me wait long, running around the corner from Main with every ounce of strength left in that old body. He wore a thick, dark blue jumpsuit and a knit hat, and under those heavy arms he towed a snow shovel and a pile of electric blankets. I threw the door open for him and scooted over, letting him into the driver's seat.

"Your car's gone," I said.

"Don't need it no more," he answered, that raspy voice exhausted from the run. "No time left. This is all I got to do now." He turned the key, and once again the plow roared to life. From the look on his face, I could tell I wasn't going to get an answer unless I pressed the issue.

He wanted the issue pressed. I had to know.

"You've known about this storm for longer than anybody else," I said. "You knew about Gus's plow. You know a lot of things that it doesn't seem like you should know."

"You're right," he answered, slamming the wheel to the right and tearing the monstrous plow down Main Street. "I been dreamin' this one for a long time. I didn't know when it was comin', but it's here now."

"But that doesn't make any sense!" I wanted to grab him by the throat and shake him.

"It don't," he answered, "but that's the way it's always been." The snow and ice were starting to accumulate on the road, but the plow shoved it aside with ease. "Did you know I got my start livin' on the street downtown with my mama?"

I shook my head. As a wrestler, Rocco was always billed as coming from the Rocky Mountains. I'd never thought to ask how much of that was true.

"When I was little, I'd have these dreams," he continued. "Dreams about things comin' down the pike. Always things I was gonna see, never anything else." He turned to me and narrowed his eyes. "Big boy like me, livin' on the streets, no money, no education, no job . . . how do you 'spose I found somebody to train me to wrestle?"

I didn't know. I just stared, gaping.

"I'd dream of the radio, tellin' me the way games turned out, and then I'd tell Kowalski, my trainer. He'd make good money bettin' on the games. And I'd get my training. And he'd show me how to do a hold or a suplex. And later on, I made them so much money that they made me champion."

Then I remembered the radio at the restaurant, that little handheld device. Always tuned into a game. Not just the Reds or the Bengals like most folks out here, but Pacers basketball and ice hockey and horse racing. He didn't dream it if he didn't experience it later on. It was insurance.

I looked deep into my old friend's eyes and saw none of the champion's confidence anymore. Rocco the wrestler was gone, and only Darryl was left. Old, broken down. Still a giant but on his last legs, like a crumbling bridge. But behind it all, the determination remained. He huffed slowly, gripping the wheel tighter.

"The Lord gave me a gift, and I used it to make myself a star," he said. "I got a lot of penance to pay. And I needed your help."

"But why?" I said. What could I say? I didn't believe for a second that he was lying. "Why me? And how'd you know my boyfriend drove a plow?"

Rocco turned to me. He smiled. I cupped my hands over my mouth with a gasp as I realized that he had dreamed the very conversation we'd just had.

"Thank you," he said. "Thank you for puttin' your confidence in an old con man like me. You're gonna get out of this just fine, I think, but I'm gonna need you to take those blankets." He motioned to the pile of electric blankets—all of them seemingly brand new—that he'd laid in the seat next to him. "We got a lot of people to pick up, and we ain't got room in here."

And so I leaned back in the seat, resting my head against the scratchy brown cloth. The snow and ice fell faster and heavier than I'd ever seen it before, and gusts of wind carried the freshly fallen flakes into drifts along the side of the road, against the edges of buildings, around the dead trees of January. In any other storm like this, I'd have been terrified.

But I was going to be okay. Rocco had seen it. I just wish, in hindsight, that I'd considered his prophecy to its logical conclusion.

***

Main Street was as empty as I'd ever seen it as we barreled south through wind and snow, stopping about once a block so Rocco could get out. The first time he stopped was outside of an empty gas station, where a boy of about twelve sat on the ground, clutching his arms against himself. Rocco stepped outside, sliding and slipping through the snow with an agility I'd never seen in the old giant before. He carried the boy to the truck, handed him an electric blanket, and helped him into the back of the truck.

"Where we going, Rocco?" I finally thought to ask.

"Hospital," he huffed, gasping for breath against the bitter cold and his own exhaustion. "Grand . . . Grandview."

And we sped off again, stopping every few blocks to pick up another poor soul. Some of them were children, young and nearly frozen in the face of the storm. Others were bent with age, burying their haggard bodies in whatever flannels and old coats they could find. Not one of them, I don't think, had a home.

When we reached a tall thin house near Philadelphia Drive—about halfway to the hospital—Rocco stopped the car and turned to me. "You gotta handle this one," he gasped. "He's a doctor. He's late."

"Me?" I asked. "Why me?"

"He's a fan," Rocco said. "I seen him at the shows. If I go up there, he'd just . . . just slow me down."

I knew what he meant. If I'd been just a normal fan and Rocco Marshall had come to my house, it'd have been hard to get going after that. So I climbed out, pulling my arm over my face as a blast of frigid air nearly flattened me. How could Rocco move through this? The only thing that kept me going toward the door was the fact that I was walking with the wind.

I didn't even knock before the door opened and a tall, spectacled man in a tie stepped through the door.

"D-d-d-d-doctor?" I said between chattering teeth, my voice nearly lost in the wind.

"I'm Dr. Phillips!" he shouted. "I've got to get to Grandview! Can you get me there?"

I motioned back to the plow, holding on to his arm as we both braced ourselves against the wind, relying on his stature to keep myself from falling over. He sat in the front—between me and Rocco—and brushed the snow from his button-up shirt.

"Don't I know you?" Dr. Phillips asked, turning to the familiar man at the wheel. "Aren't you Rocco—"

"Name's Darryl," Rocco grunted. "I drive a plow."

***

Between the stops and the wind, it had been nearly an hour before we turned onto Forest Avenue towards Grandview. The snow hadn't piled high in the street, but it was drifting tall and thick. Dr. Phillips and I sat in the front; fourteen others sat in the back, huddled under electric blankets to shield themselves against the storm. There was only one blanket left.

Rocco stopped near the corner at an old brick house, where the snow had blown nearly four feet up the side of the building. This time, Rocco left the truck with his shovel, and he went straight for the snow, carefully shoveling aside as much as he could. I watched the freshly shoveled snow blow against his jumpsuit, into his face, dusting it with white. Soon, he reached his hand into the drift and produced a person covered in powder: an old man, bent and gaunt, his dark skin speckled with snow and ice. He was unconscious, and Rocco carried him to the front of the truck instead of the back.

"He's okay, isn't he?" Rocco said quickly, a desperate look in his eyes as he stared at Dr. Phillips.

The doctor felt his pulse, checked his breathing, and nodded incredulously. He had seen some incredible things today, and Rocco took the old man to the back, draping the electric blanket over him.

Dr. Phillips watched through the window separating the cabin from the truck bed. "How'd he know that guy was there?" he asked.

With a shrug, I said, "He must have seen something move." A lie. Kayfabe.

***

By the time we reached Grandview a few minutes later, fifteen souls in need of medical attention and one cardiologist were ready to be taken inside. It was approaching late morning when we got them all inside, and the storm was fiercer than ever before. It was Rocco who was slowing down, gasping for air as I led him by the arm back to the truck. When he sat down inside the truck, he looked like he needed to head back inside to the hospital.

"You okay, big man?" I asked, clasping a gloved hand on his knee. "You did good. You saved lives tonight."

"We . . . we gotta take this plow back," he gasped. "Your boyfriend's gonna be home soon."

"You think so?" I asked, and Rocco turned his head to shoot me a sideways glare. "Yeah, you think so. You okay to drive?"

He threw the car into drive. "Gotta be."

***

He wasn't. Compared to our harrowing drive south down Main Street, saving trapped soul after trapped soul, our trip back was a trudge, the snow and ice still yielding before the massive plow, the winds still buffeting its sides to no avail. Rocco was in no hurry to finish the trek, and I couldn't blame him. I'd seen him as a role model to a lot of kids in this area, but this was the first time I saw him be a real hero.

There was relief in those old eyes, his eyebrows and hair flecked with snowflakes, making him appear still more ancient. But that wasn't all. His hands were shaking, and his posture wasn't steady. Dr. Phillips had been worried about his state by the time we picked up our twelfth person, but I didn't really feel like listening. I think I knew. I know for a fact Rocco knew.

So it came as no surprise to me that, when we finally—after another two hours—turned the plow onto Englewood Dam, a beast of a black pickup truck turned, blocking both lanes.

Gus's pickup.

I looked up at Rocco. "Damn it," I managed to spit out. "What now?"

Rocco didn't answer. He parked the car, dropping his hands to his side, slowly unbuckling his seat belt.

The door to the pick-up flew open, and Gus stomped out, boots pulled over his sweat pants, his thick face hidden behind a black ski mask. "What the *hell* do you think you're doing?" he shouted, his voice audible through the windows, over the din of the storm. "That's my plow!"

He only wore one glove. The other glove held a silver Smith & Wesson pistol covered with wet drops of snow.

"You think you're gonna take my jobs?" Gus screamed. "Who do you think you are? You're—"

He stopped suddenly, jaw dropping nearly to the ground. "Sherri?"

"Oh, God," I muttered, burying my face into my arms.

"Don't you hide from me! I know it's you in there! In there with that wrestler, aren't you?"

Rocco had managed to push the door open, shoving it open with his shoulder. As he ambled out of the truck, his left hand dropped, and with his right he clutched onto his chest.

"I see what this is!" Gus shouted. "You two tryin' to mess with me again! Well, I got you now! You stole my plow, and I'm in the mood for a little *justice*!"

He raised the gun.

"Gus, no!" I shrieked.

But as I dove toward the door, a fresh gust of wind caught Gus's arms, and the single shot in the gun fired far to the right, over the edge of the dam. At the crack of the pistol, Rocco's knees seemed to buckle, and he fell to the ground, still clutching his chest.

Gus gaped, watching as I slid out of the car and looked him over. I could see the glazed over look in Rocco's eyes, and he gurgled and gasped against the cold.

"He's having a heart attack!" I shouted. "Get help!"

"But—but you guys stole my plow!"

"You get help this second or I'll find something sharp and steal something else!"

And all at once Gus found his hustle, sliding toward the snow plow and helping Rocco back into the middle seat. He backed his truck onto the side of the road, then hurried back to the snow plow and into the driver's seat.

"You're going to jail, you know," Gus said. "I don't give a damn if he has a heart attack or not. You stole my plow and you're going to jail."

"We saved fifteen people tonight," I said, fighting back tears. "We did more for this town than you've done in your life. And you've got a man in your car that's dying right now and if you don't pour everything into helping him then you're the most miserable—"

"I ain't dyin'."

I turned with a start. Rocco's eyes were open, his lips upturned. But he still trembled, his voice still weak.

"Can't keep me down," he gasped. "Can't do it. I'm bigger than that. You bring that Grim Reaper over here and I'll stomp—" He coughed—a loud, raucous cough. "I'll stomp his teeth into that skull of his."

"You did good, Rocco," I answered, one more time taking his hand. His enormous mitt took mine, still enveloping it, but weakly, feebly.

"*Mon cheri*," he said, one last time. All wrong. And he leaned back again, the smile never fading even as his breath left him.

***

Of course he didn't make it; he was dead before we made it to the hospital. And of course Gus didn't press charges; cowards never follow through on threats like that. I stayed at the hospital for two days until I could catch a bus back up town. There was no way I was riding with Gus again.

The bus ride home seemed to last years, and I stared out the window, watching people shovel their driveways, watching the snow plows clear out parking lots. All I could think about was Rocco, that last smile, the way he'd willingly given it all to help those people that last night.

And yet I was taken back to that night long ago, when I first met Rocco. I remembered him rubbing my hair, smiling at me, putting that big warm hand on my shoulder. I think when I look back on it now, I can see the sadness behind those eyes. He had known it. He had dreamed of it before.

"You're gonna break somebody's heart someday, kid," he had said. The darkness beneath the words pierces my memory. But at the time, all I saw was the champion's smile. Kayfabe.

MEET THE
AUTHORS AND EDITORS

Gery L. Deer

EXECUTIVE EDITOR, CO-FOUNDER, DIRECTOR

Gery L. Deer is the executive editor and co-founder of the Western Ohio Writers Association and the developer of *Flights of Fiction*. He is an entrepreneur, freelance commercial and feature writer, editor, and an expert contributor to television and print media. Since selling his first piece of freelance journalism in 1987, his career has spanned every form of content including his weekly op-ed column, *Deer In Headlines*, which has appeared weekly in the *Xenia Daily Gazette* and online since 2008. In 2010, his feature story series titled, *Be All You Can Be* earned nominations for a Pulitzer Prize in journalism and the Ohio Public Image Network Media Award. Since 2006, Gery has been a freelance feature writer for virtually every major media franchise in the greater Dayton market including the *Dayton Daily News, Springfield News-Sun*, and *Ohio Community Media Group* publications. Since February of 2012, he has served as a contributor to the WDTN–Channel 2 daytime television talk show, *Living Dayton*.

Barbara Huiner Deer

EDITORIAL COMMITTEE, CO-FOUNDER

Originally from the Chicago area, Barbara Huiner Deer is co-founder and a senior editorial committee member of the Western Ohio Writers Association. She earned a bachelor's degree in social work from Calvin College in Grand Rapids, Michigan and writes short and novel -length young adult fiction. She enjoys reading and fitness and spends her spare time with her husband Gery and son Henry.

Michael Martin
THE DEAD OF WINTER
Michael Martin has been spinning stories as long as he can remember. This included recruiting family members to type as he dictated, until they finally just bought him his own damn typewriter. He works as a marketing drone for an Ohio-based manufacturing company, and lives in Dayton near his immensely talented and beautiful daughters. "Dead of Winter" is his first published piece of fiction. Michael is a member of the WOWA Editorial Committee, a co-organizer of the group and designer of the organization's logo.

Dennis L. Hitzeman
ST. GEORGE AND THE DRAGON
Dennis L Hitzeman is a hopeful writer from the Dayton, Ohio area. His favorite genre is tales of the strange. In addition to writing short stories, novels, and non-fiction pieces for print and the web, he also runs a family-owned, sustainable farm, roasts coffee, and does information technology consulting.

Tammy Newsom
DEAR MR. CHANEY
Tammy Newsom is a longtime resident of Dayton, Ohio. After the *Dayton Daily News* ceased accepting short story submissions, she began developing her voice in speculative fiction. Tammy currently owns and operates a hospitality recruiting franchise out of her home office, to place restaurant and hotel managers in new careers.

Arch Little II
A CHICK STORY
Arch Little returned to his birthplace of Dayton, Ohio in 2003 after retiring from the U.S. Army. He is married to his wonderful wife Helga and has two lovely daughters and three young grandsons. Humor is a very important part of Arch's life and he enjoys adding it to his writing.

Lynda Sappington

LISA GOODMAN, WRITER

Lynda Sappington writes fantasy, humor, adventure, some romance, a little horror or suspense at times. Her stories usually are characterized by humor, whimsy and adventure (depending on the story) and characters who often are "characters." She has two published fantasy novels and a published how-to book on sculpting, now in its second edition.

Philip A. Lee

NOSE ART

A freelance writer and editor, Philip A. Lee has published several short stories on BattleCorps.com and has written gaming books for Catalyst Game Labs. He lives in Dayton, Ohio, with his significant other and three cats. Philip is a member of the WOWA Editorial Committee and a co-organizer of the group. You can learn more about his work at www.philipleewriting.com.

Liz Coley

SYNTHETIC INTEGRATED RATIONAL INTELLIGENCE

Some people are born writers but Liz Coley says she was a born reader. A biochemistry major at Yale, she took a British Literature class as an excuse to read for pleasure outside her curriculum. She continued through the years to hone her craft through workshops and associations with fellow writers. In 2010 and 2011, six of her short stories were published followed by her independent young adult novel, *Out of Xibalba*. Her first internationally published novel, *Pretty Girl 13*, released through Katherine Tegen at HarperCollins, is available now. More at www.lizcoley.com.

Deanna Newsom

TABITHA'S PORTRAIT

Deanna Newsom moved to Ohio from Canada in 2008, and wondered how she'd survived so long without seeing a redbud tree in bloom.

She wrote "Tabitha's Portrait" to explore the vulnerability of motherhood and the secret hopes and disappointments that burden even the plainest of lives. She lives in Yellow Springs with her family.

Kate Seagraves

BIRD WATCHING

Kate Seegraves is a former print journalist whose work has appeared in newspapers and magazines in Texas and Ohio. She currently works in Columbus, Ohio as an editor for a Fortune 100 company. She lives in Springfield with her husband Chris and their son Noah. Kate is a member of the WOWA Editorial Committee and a co-organizer of the group.

LD Masterson

MOTIVE

Born in Boston, and a diehard Red Sox fan, LD Masterson lived on both coasts before becoming landlocked in Ohio. After twenty years keeping the computers up and running for the American Red Cross, she now divides her time between writing and serving the whims of a neurotic Jack Russell terrier named Sophie. LD writes mystery and suspense and is a proud member of Mystery Writers of America, Sisters in Crime, and the Western Ohio Writers Association. Read more online at http://ldmasterson-author.blogspot.com.

Bill Bicknell

KAYFABE

Bill Bicknell has been an avid writer since fourth grade and an avid wrestling fan for nearly that long as well. His comedy stories have appeared in the local publication *MudRock: Stories and Tales*. Bill is a faculty member at Sinclair Community College and Wright State University, where he teaches English. He lives in New Lebanon, Ohio, with his wife and two children. Bill is a member of the WOWA Editorial Committee and a co-organizer of the group.

The WOWA Editors

Western Ohio Writers Association Editorial Committee 2013
(From Left) Bill Bicknell, Philip A. Lee, Michael Martin,
Gery L. Deer, Barbara Huiner Deer, Kate Seegraves

Thanks for reading!
To learn more about the Western Ohio Writers Association,
please visit our website at www.westernohiowriters.org.